LEGACY

by Neil Somerville

Copyright © 2022 Neil Somerville

All rights reserved.

The characters and events portrayed in this book are fictitious. Any similarity to real persons, living or dead, is coincidental and not intended by the author.

No part of this book may be reproduced, or stored in a retrieval system, or transmitted in any form or by any means, electronic, mechanical, photocopying, recording, or otherwise, without express written permission of the author or his representatives.

To Thalia
Thank you for your wonderful legacy.

*Our deeds create
the seeds of
our tomorrow.*

Neil Somerville

Scurra 1832

No one was going to miss this.

Despite the flurries of snow and biting north wind, they all turned out. Young and old, muffled in thick coats, scarves and hats, they all made their way to the prison. There had not been a hanging on Scurra for three years and, unlike the last time – when it was a drunk from the mainland – this was someone most knew: twenty-year-old Mary Hunter. Mary came from one of the most respected families on the island, but the Hunter name and influence meant nothing. She had been convicted of murder and was sentenced to hang. And if, as the posters had declared, her neck was not broken by the shock of the fall, the Moral Teacher would pull the legs of the miserable girl until by his weight and strength he strangled her.

The islanders huddled together on the cobbled square, gazing in awe at the tall instrument of death that had been erected earlier that morning. They waited patiently and the few who spoke talked in hushed whispers. The snow continued to fall, casting a virginal beauty over the grim surroundings.

At 11 o'clock, just as the clock on Narraport church began its first stroke, the prison doors swung open and Mary Hunter was escorted out.

Wearing a brown tunic, she looked pale and haggard, far removed from the time – just months ago – when she was a joyous young beauty with everything to live for. She glanced across the assembled multitude. Many she recognised but there was no friendliness in their faces now. They just stared at her – watching and waiting.

She mounted the snow-covered steps of the scaffold and stood while the Moral Teacher secured her hands. At this point many had chosen to speak their last words, to plead for forgiveness and sometimes admit to their crimes, but Mary Hunter remained silent. There was no more for her to say.

The Moral Teacher placed the rope around her neck and a cap over her eyes, obliterating the light for ever.

As she stood there on the scaffold she said a prayer quietly to herself. And waited.

Later that day Mary Hunter's body was placed in irons and taken to Gibbet Hill where it hung as a deterrent to all. The body remained on the gibbet for five days, constantly buffeted by the winds and frequent snow showers. On the fifth day her family, acting without authority, cut the body down, removed the irons and buried the body at a secret location.

With the removal of the body the islanders thought that this was the end of a tragic incident in the history of the island. But it was not the end. It was the beginning of a legacy.

The legacy of Mary Hunter.

1

Scurra 1989

Captain Engelman stared out of the rain-splattered windows at the decks below. Passengers were still coming aboard: parties of schoolchildren, families about to start their holidays, students, couples young and old; on they all clambered shouting and waving, cheery despite the weather. It was Scurra's busiest time. Three-quarters of the island's revenue came from tourism and most people travelled over on one of the three Scurra ferries.

Today the ferry was going to be late. Yes, there were rough seas and high winds, but it was the passengers who held things up, not the cars or lorries. The loading had been completed on time. There were just so many people on foot.

Down on the lower decks there was a flurry of activity. Mr Robson's class had commandeered a corner of the lounge and thirty noisy nine-year-olds, many away from home for the first time, were laughing, joking and talking excitedly about the week ahead. Mr Robson and two other teachers sat with the children, oblivious to the commotion. Families were sitting in small clusters, grappling with their bulging hand luggage and extricating themselves from their clinging wet clothes. A large queue had already formed in front of the cafe and bar.

Leif Olsen, cold, wet and bedraggled, took one look at the crowded lounge and turned away. He headed towards one of the smaller sitting areas, but they were also occupied. Without waterproofs only the most foolhardy would venture out onto one of the open decks.

Leif looked around. Several other students were squatting where they could, in between the litter bins, drink and game machines. Finding an empty space, Leif propped his rucksack against a wall and settled against his makeshift back rest.

Once settled, Leif dried his face and little goatee beard with his handkerchief, then closed his eyes. It had been a long day in a long and tiring week. And despite the noise, the activity and excited voices, Leif fell asleep.

A sharp tap on his right shoulder woke him and to his surprise saw a smartly dressed young woman crouching in front of him.

'Excuse me,' she began. 'You're about to lose your wallet.'

Horrified, Leif looked down and saw his wallet balanced precariously between the folds of his damp denim jacket. Leif pushed it firmly back in his inside pocket and looked back at the passenger. 'Thanks, I'd have been sunk without it.'

The young woman smiled and returned to a tall man waiting for her. Unlike most of the other passengers he was wearing a suit and carrying an attaché case. His thick brown hair was immaculately brushed back.

'Come, my dear,' he said abruptly, taking the young woman's arm. As he turned to lead his companion away, the man cast a brief and disdainful look at Leif.

Leif watched him guide the young lady into the dining area, amused rather than annoyed at his reaction. For the rest of the journey he held on to his wallet through the folds of his jacket and this time he didn't dare sleep. At any rate, there was too much going on around him, plus the scare of all the holiday money he had so nearly lost.

One of the youngsters announced the first sighting of Scurra with a yell of excitement.

'Land!' he cried. 'Look, look, it's there!' and pointed to an indistinct blur just visible through a steamy porthole.

'Will all drivers and car passengers please make their way to the car deck,' boomed a recorded message over the tannoy. 'Will all foot passengers . . . '

Leif struggled to his feet and slipped his rucksack back on his shoulders. He checked his wallet was still in place and glancing over the space he had occupied made sure there was nothing left behind. Then he followed the other foot passengers down the steps to the disembarkation point. Mr Robson stood at the bottom of the stairs shouting commands to his class. No one bothered to listen.

The engines quietened and for one, maybe two minutes, the ferry seemed to drift. The engines suddenly started up for a moment. There were shouts from outside. A jolt. Passenger knocked against passenger. Then the ferry steadied and became still.

'Make way,' shouted a crew member, and two of them forced their way through the waiting throng to the disembarkation point. Then the doors slid open and the passengers lurched forward onto the sodden gangways of the Scurra Ferry Company.

Leif, buffeted and jostled, found himself propelled out of the ferry and onto Scurra. The rain had stopped, and the air was cool and fresh. Leif gave up his ticket and saw the rows of taxis, courtesy coaches and an open-topped bus waiting for the passengers. Mr Robson and his class, together with another school party, headed for the bus.

Turning, Leif made his way along the pier. Vehicles, many laden with cases and bulging roof racks, started to drive off the ferry and slowly make their way onto the Scurra roads. An emerald Rolls Royce passed Leif. In the front passenger seat, a dignified, elderly man was staring straight ahead. Next to him, at the wheel, was the disapproving young man who had given Leif such a look of disgust. In the seat behind him sat the young woman who had told him about his wallet. Whether she recognised him or not Leif was unsure, but she stared out of the window at him. And through the splattered windows of the car, he thought she looked fearful and afraid. As if Scurra was the last place she really wanted to be.

2

Katherine Strevans put the phone down and called through to the office behind her.

'It's arrived.'

Norman Strevans glanced up from the accounts he was studying.

'What?'

'The ferry. It's arrived. They'll be here soon.'

'Right.' Norman nodded and returned to his work.

'Well, aren't you going to do anything?' snapped his wife.

'I thought it was all done.'

Katherine Strevans took a deep breath, glared at her husband, strode across the lobby and up the stairs. She wondered how he could be calm. The most important guests they'd ever had and there he was sitting nonchalantly in the office. It was an honour to have the Tyler's staying. And a bonus to have the Dickens Suite occupied in the peak weeks at peak prices.

Katherine unlocked the door of the Dickens Suite and entered. The name had been chosen because, according to local history, Dickens had spent a night at the hotel, although none of the surviving guest books had ever confirmed the fact – but it added some glamour.

The suite was immaculate. Ann Walker, the cleaner, had done an excellent job. There was an eye-catching display of sweet peas on the coffee table and the new furnishings, bought at considerable expense, gave the room an entirely new elegance. The windows had been thoroughly cleaned and the view out towards Little Scurra Bay was stunning.

Looking at her watch, she hurried through to the largest of the three bedrooms. This would be Sir Alec Tyler's room. Everything was ready. Drink facilities, new television, personal phone, rocking chair – she had done her homework and knew that Sir Alec had a fondness for rocking chairs – and with a selection of newspapers and glossy upmarket magazines on the coffee table. Some volumes of Dickens were prominently displayed in the small bookcase because she'd also read that Sir Alec had once compared his life to that of Dickens – from an impoverished start to a position of prominence and self-created wealth. The en suite bathroom was spotless.

Hurrying through to the next bedroom, she smoothed the top of the blue duvet. Again, everything was in order, everything prepared to the highest standards and, Katherine was sure, up to the standards that Edward Harrison, Sir Alec's secretary and business advisor, expected.

The third bedroom was the smallest. This would be where Juliet Tyler would sleep. Decorated in pastel pink, the room had commanding views of the lush fields of Hunter's Valley and the downs beyond. Katherine pulled one of the velvet curtains straight and with a tissue removed a dead fly from the windowsill.

Ann had put an arrangement of roses on the dressing table. One of the flowers looked askew. Katherine straightened it only to find some petals falling away in her hand. Deftly she plucked the dying flower from the arrangement and left the room. They would be here at any moment.

Leif Olsen had studied the directions to the campsite the night before. From the harbour it was either the No 12 bus or, if using your own transport, followed the Lower Arch road. The campsite was before Lower Arch and as it was just five miles away, Leif decided to walk.

After leaving the harbour, passing a parade of gift shops and countless guest houses, the road left the town and began to twist and climb through forestry commission land. There were some parking places along the route, several picnic sites and plenty of marked footpaths. At one point some workmen were cutting down storm-damaged trees and nodded to Leif as he passed.

At the top of the hill, Leif adjusted his rucksack and wiped the sweat from his brow. His clothes, spare shoes and tent weighed heavily. He felt tempted to stop but he wanted to get to the campsite and set up his home for the next two weeks – or however long his money lasted. He preferred not to think what would have happened had he lost his wallet. The young woman on the ferry had literally saved his holiday.

Leif continued along the road until he came to a small white bungalow. Outside was a bucket containing bunches of freesias for sale and trays of newly picked vegetables, some with damp soil still clinging to their roots. Leif bought a lettuce, cucumber and bag of tomatoes, leaving the money in a rusty biscuit tin.

As he started off again an open-topped bus passed him and on the top deck he saw some of the schoolchildren that had been on the ferry. At the back of the bus was one of the teachers. The bus slowed, indicated and then turned down an unmade road.

Edward Harrison ignored the sign to the car park and parked opposite the steps of the Scurra Manor Hotel.

Sir Alec Tyler looked approvingly at the hotel. It had style, character and history. The white frontage had been freshly painted and almost shimmered in the sun that had now broken through. The rose borders at the front were well tended and the freshly mown grass smelt lush.

Sir Alec eased himself out of the car. At seventy-four he was no longer the agile youth who had once clambered over the Scurra downs.

'My stick, please.'

Juliet passed her father his stick from the back of the car.

'So, what do you think?'

Juliet looked at her father, a little surprised to be asked her opinion so soon. 'It's lovely, Dad, quite homely,' she replied.

'It'll do, I suppose,' declared Edward, slamming the driver's door.

The front door of the hotel opened and Katherine Strevans, with a carefully rehearsed smile, descended the two steps to the car. Her husband hovered in the background, his interest focused on the car rather than his guests.

'How lovely to see you. I do hope you had a good journey.'

'Thank you, we did,' replied Sir Alec, advancing to shake Katherine's hand.

'Do come this way. I'll get you to sign the visitor's book and show you to the Dickens Suite. I am sure you'll like it here.'

The three followed their hostess up the steps and Juliet stumbled slightly on the paving. Edward Harrison reached over and put his arm around her in what seemed a protective gesture. The young woman stiffened slightly at his touch.

'Are you okay?' He bent towards her, looking into her face with a little smile.

She refused to look at him and shrugged him off. 'I'm fine, thanks.'

Fifteen minutes later they were installed in the suite. Harrison, having already set up his hefty laptop on the dressing table, began to unpack, while Sir Alec sat admiring the views of Little Scurra Bay and Juliet stood at the window of her small but well-appointed room.

She looked out over the undulating fields of

Hunter's valley, so different from the bustle of the city life she knew so well. Everything on Scurra appeared so clean, so fresh. And not so far away were the downs that ran through the middle of island. While her father and Edward Harrison were playing golf, she would walk the downs, taking her sketch pad with her. She looked forward to it.

Juliet heard the door click behind her. It was probably her father. Or Edward. She was annoyed her father had asked him to come. Edward was conceited, arrogant and pompous – and didn't hide the fact that he was attracted to her. He may be her father's friend and advisor but she neither liked nor trusted him.

Juliet turned, surprised to see no one there. But she noticed a petal had just come away from one of the roses and watched as it spiralled its way down to the floor.

3

Leif Olsen knocked at the front door of the Bush Retreat, a ramshackle building belonging to the owners of the campsite.

A tall, awkward youth sporting an orange T-shirt opened the door. He took Leif's name and mumbled something about getting Mum. Leif eased the rucksack from off his shoulders and waited.

A few moments later a pleasingly rotund woman with flour and jam splattered on her plastic apron appeared at the door.

'*Velkommen til* Bush *campingplass*,' she said, then added with a laugh, 'Oh, I do hope I got that right. I asked Joe Thorpe. He speaks Norwegian, you know. I told him I had a Norwegian coming and he told me what to say.'

'Good try,' said Leif, amused. 'But I'm English. I got my name from my father who was a Dane.'

'Oh lor, trust me to get it all wrong! Anyway, I'm Rose Bush, a name you'll never forget. Thorny but nice, that's what I say! But you can call me Rose. Anything you want, just ask for me. You've met Billy. He's my son. And Thomas is my husband. And mind you call him Thomas though. He gets real cross if he's called Tom.'

'I'll remember that,' replied Leif, already warming to Rose. She was very much like one of his aunts, a touch eccentric but motherly.

'Anyhow,' she continued, 'you'll be wanting to put up your tent, I guess.'

Leif nodded.

'Well, we have four fields. We've got a party of schoolchildren in one of them. Thomas is with them at the moment. Another field we have for caravans. Then there's another field with quite a few families in it, but if you want a bit of peace and quiet, I suggest you go to the fourth field. It's the furthest one away. And I suggest you camp at the top of the field. It can get a bit soggy at the bottom.' Rose paused, casually brushing some flour from her apron. 'And when you've got your tent up, come back here and I'll give you some odds and ends to get you started. And there's a post office and shop on the road to Lower Arch.'

'Thank you.' Leif turned to go.

'And don't forget,' added Rose. 'It's the fourth field. Just keep going along the track as far as you can. It's the field with the slope. It's called Gibbet Field.'

'*Gibbet* Field? What, like you mean a hangman's gibbet?' Leif turned and stared at her.

'Oh yes, my duck,' said Rose with a solemn nod, 'And there's a good view of the gibbet from there, but you won't mind that, will you?'

Gibbet Field was small and mostly enclosed by hedgerow. The grass had been newly cut and several areas were lighter in colour than the rest – the sites of previous campers. The field was on a gentle slope and beyond the far hedge the downs rose sharply, with the gibbet standing proud and stark at the highest point. Leif stood and stared at it for some time and felt a little uneasy. He had never seen such a thing before. Why, he wondered, was it still here, in this day and age? He shrugged and decided it was one of those grisly reminders of the past that had for some reason been preserved.

Choosing a flat area near the top of the field, he quickly set up his tent. He had used it many times before and had spent the previous night sticking plasters over tears in the ground sheet. Once the tent was up, he unrolled his sleeping bag, unpacked his navy guernsey and some crumpled sweatshirts. They would serve him well over his stay, both for warmth and as pillows. Then he set up his camping stove, collapsible water bottle and cooking pans, such as they were, outside the tent. Zipping up the tent door, he stretched out on his sleeping bag. After the early start of the morning and the frenzy of the last few weeks, he felt weary. There had been the final exams to contend with, the parties, the farewells, and now . . . now, until the results came out, he could rest, unwind and think. A fortnight on Scurra would do him good.

It had been fifteen years since his last visit and the memory of it had stayed with him all that time. It was the last holiday he was to have with his father and a happy one. He was six then, and he remembered how his parents had taken him to Pear Beach and how he'd buried his father in the sand. Then, amid all the hilarity, his father woke and feigned surprise at the amount of sand Leif had heaped on him. With much exaggerated panting and groaning, his Dad had struggled up and shaken the sand away. Later, he'd taken Leif to a blue and white ice cream kiosk and bought some choc ices. Those were such happy times, destined to end so abruptly.

Within a week of getting home, Peter Olsen was taken ill and was dead just a few days later. His last words to Leif were, *'Du kan gore det, min son, du kan gore det.' You can do it, my son, you can do it*. His dad had always had high hopes for Leif and he owed it to him to do well. And this return visit to Scurra was like a pilgrimage to the memory of Peter Olsen.

4

Ann Walker, the housekeeper at the Scurra Manor Hotel, also helped in the kitchen on a Saturday night. It allowed some of the other staff an evening off and brought her a little extra money.

Ann had been at the hotel for fifteen years and enjoyed the atmosphere of hotel life. It was forever changing. New visitors arriving, others departing. And although she mainly worked behind the scenes, she often met the guests, including sometimes the famous ones.

Scurra Manor Hotel had a fine reputation and was probably the best of the privately-run hotels on Scurra, but she knew it was hard to maintain. Katherine Strevans had often spoken of her 'special plans' for the place, but there was never the money or Norman was not willing.

Norman had lived in the hotel all his life. His grandparents had originally bought it in 1923, then his parents had taken it over and when his father had become crippled with arthritis, Norman finally took charge. Whether he was happy in his role as hotelier, Ann was never sure. Maybe he would have done better as an accountant, a solicitor or in an office job. The socializing and pandering that went with hotel life was just not Norman's style. Katherine loved it though, especially when there were distinguished guests staying.

And the Tylers were certainly important. A real coup for the hotel. Ann had only seen the Rolls and the back of Sir Alec Tyler as he made his way to the bar, but she hoped to see more of him during his stay. Perhaps even meet him. She had often read about him in the papers. He was rich but philanthropic. It was in the news only last month that he had paid for that little girl with heart problems to go to America for treatment.

Ann had heard that his daughter seemed a nice young woman. Long dark hair and a nice slim figure, as Norman Strevans described her. He didn't care for the abrupt and fussy man with them, though. It seemed, from what Norman had told her, that he had every intention of turning his bedroom into an office. He even had one of those new mobile phone things with him. But he'd have a job getting a signal here on Scurra. There were no masts or anything remotely modern in the place. It was one of the reasons people liked to come here to get away from all that technology stuff.

'Have to put up with the room telephone like everyone else,' shrugged Norman. 'The man's supposed to be on holiday, isn't he?'

Katherine breezed into the kitchen. She was in a mauve evening dress, the sequins shimmering in the light. Norman had often called Katherine the Sparkler, and that evening she sparkled.

'Good evening, Ann,' said Katherine brightly.

She was heavily made up. With the right colours and some deft strokes Katherine had a happy knack of taking years off her age.

'You look superb,' complimented Ann.

'Thank you. Is everything all right?'

'Yes, all fine.'

'You did a good job in the Dickens Suite. It looked marvellous and . . .' Katherine moved closer to Ann and added in a conspiratorial whisper, 'I think they're impressed. They're used to only the best, you know.'

Norman wandered into the kitchen, obviously uncomfortable in a dinner jacket and bow tie. He cast a look at Katherine and blinked. Ann tried not to smile. Norman was, as always, suitably dazzled by his wife.

'You look absolutely . . .' He tried to peck her on the cheek.

'Come on, Norman,' cut in Katherine, 'no time for that. Get up those stairs. The guests will be coming down at any moment.'

'Yes, dear,' and as Norman turned he winked at Ann.

Katherine went over to see the chef, Paul Chase. He was setting out some of the entrées and Katherine cast an approving glance.

Ann looked at her watch. She knew any moment the first orders would be coming and Paul – a competent chef and the best they'd hired for a long time – would be thrown into his nightly panic. He was always keen to impress and was especially so tonight with the Tylers dining at the hotel.

Edward Harrison looked around the dining room.

'Mmm . . .quaint,' he declared. He felt like adding that it was grossly inferior to anywhere else he'd stayed in recent years but wisely knew that would offend Sir Alec. The Scurra Manor Hotel was Sir Alec's own choice. And despite an attempt at gentle persuasion, for once he had failed to get Sir Alec to change his mind. For some reason the old man was set on coming and determined that both he and Juliet accompany him.

Edward glanced across at Sir Alec, a hint of a smile crossing his otherwise inscrutable face. Maybe Sir Alec, wily old fellow that he was, was playing matchmaker. Perhaps he hoped that the daughter born to him so late in life might wed Edward, the son he wished he'd had.

Edward was very attracted to Juliet. She was fresh, innocent and graceful. Her wealth seemed unimportant to her and she lived a quiet life in her unassuming little London flat. Tonight, in her dark blue evening dress with a silver crucifix hanging from her neck, she looked charming without being ostentatious. Old Sir Alec was right – on this holiday they would have more time together, be free from the pressures of London and he would have more time to win her heart. So far, she didn't seem responsive, but he felt supremely confident that he would win her over. Edward wanted Juliet and he always got what he wanted.

Norman Strevans approached the table and gave a slight bow.

'Is everything to your satisfaction?' he enquired.

Sir Alec smiled. He had a happy knack of smiling. Even when he lay desperately ill in hospital he always managed a warm and confident smile. 'The prawns were delicious. Are they local?'

'Indeed, sir. Scurra has a good reputation for prawns. Among the finest in the country.'

'Is that so?' mused Sir Alec. 'I'll remember that.'

Norman beamed as he entered the kitchen.

'You look happy,' observed Ann, wiping a smear from a dinner plate.

'Oh, I am,' declared the hotelier.

'And Sir Alec is happy?'

'Perfect. In his element.'

'And Mr Harrison?'

Norman Strevans shrugged his shoulders. 'Who can tell? Bit of a weird fish if you ask me. Mind you, got a lot of hair. I'll have to ask him the secret.'

'Are you sure it's not a wig?'

'If it is, it's fooled me.'

'And what about Miss Tyler?'

'Fine,' declared Norman, adding with a cheesy smile, 'A lovely girl. Just like you.'

Ann Walker laughed. 'Flattery will get you nowhere.'

Ann continued inspecting the dinner plates. She was looking forward to seeing Juliet Tyler. She had heard she was quite a talented artist and had recently won an award for illustrating a children's book. Maybe she would go out and make some sketches on Scurra.

Ann suddenly thought of the room upstairs, Juliet's room. Ann had always liked the room with its pleasant views and pastel colouring. But she had heard there were some who would not enter the room. They said there was something odd about it. What, she never knew, but they had steadfastly refused to go in. Ann, however, had no misgivings and, as the orders started to come through, put all thoughts of Juliet Tyler's room out of her mind.

5

The Compass was a squat sixteenth-century pub. Buckled and cracked tiles clung precariously to an uneven roof while the white stone walls bulged as if the building had at one time been squashed by some superior weight. Under the small leaden windows hung rusty window boxes containing a mixture of trailing lobelia and fuchsias.

A weathered sign depicting a ship's compass stood in front of the pub, gently buffeted by a slight breeze.

Inside the lounge bar, long discarded lobster pots and ships lanterns hung from the low beamed ceiling and photographs of wrecks were arranged haphazardly on the walls. A ship's figurehead, a buxom woman, stood proudly in the corner of the bar and a recording of sea shanties played faintly in the background.

When Leif entered he saw a young couple at one of the tables, whispering and giggling. At another table was an old weather-worn woman, her craggy face bearing the scars of a lifetime spent out of doors. The brown cardigan she wore over her discoloured dress was patched, and a bulging Sainsbury's carrier bag was propped against the table. In front of her was a half empty tankard of beer and a crumpled crisp packet.

She looked at Leif as he crossed to the bar, her dark stony eyes following his every step. Leif was aware of her gaze and returned the look with a cheery smile. The old woman just stared back, expressionless.

Leif perched on one of the barstools and helped himself to some dry roasted peanuts from a bowl. He glanced at the chalked menu hung on the wall.

The owner of the Compass, Martin Mainwaring, came through from the public bar. He was a large man, his bulging midriff quivering with his every step. He had a ruddy complexion and a mass of curly greying hair. His right hand sported a faded tattoo of a compass.

'Evening,' he grunted.

'Evening,' replied Leif, and he gave his order. Mainwaring scribbled down his abbreviation for a cheddar Ploughman's and poured him a glass of scrumpy.

'Staying round 'ere?' he asked.

'At Bush campsite.'

'Oh, right,' grunted the publican. 'Met Billy Bush yet?'

Leif nodded. 'Briefly.'

The barman put the glass of scrumpy before Leif, slopping some of the golden liquid over the side, and pointed to a notice on the wall.

> Folk at The Compass
> Every Friday 8pm.
> Featuring the Bush Rangers.

'Billy's in that,' Mainwaring said. 'Damn fine he is too. Trouble is, he's got no ambition. Mind you, few round here have. That's the trouble with this place. Everyone expects everything on a plate.'

'I might come to it,' said Leif. 'I like folk evenings, as long as it's not one where you're expected to join in.'

'Nah, you're safe,' grunted Mainwaring and took Leif's order through to the kitchen. Moments later he returned to the bar and poured himself a pint of bitter.

'Stayin' 'ere long?' he asked.

'Two weeks. If the money lasts.'

Martin Mainwaring nodded approvingly. 'Two weeks is a good time. Too many comes over for a week. Even just a day. Can't see the island in that time.' Mainwaring raised his voice. 'Isn't that so, Ma?'

Leif turned. The old woman still sat there, the beer

in her tankard a little lower. She ignored the publican, her eyes still fixed on Leif.

Getting no reaction, Mainwaring turned back to Leif and sighed. 'In breeding,' he whispered. The publican downed half his pint. 'So,' he said, wiping the froth from his mouth. 'Will you be walking much?'

'Hope to, if the weather holds.'

'There's some nice walks in Hunter's Valley. That's not far from here. And it's nice on the downs. Past the gibbet and along the top. See for miles up there.'

'I want to get up there. And go to Pear Beach.'

'Not if I was you.' The publican shook his head and downed the rest of his pint. 'Put damned amusements all along the front. All the kids go there. No, give that a miss. Albright Beach is much nicer and,' he added with a smile, 'you get the naturists there. See some real beauts, you do.'

A peroxide blonde came through from the kitchen, carrying Leif's order. For culinary niceties whoever prepared it needed some training but for value it was unmatched. A large chunk of cheese, a small round lettuce that looked as if it just had its roots cut off and dumped on the plate, two plum tomatoes, a hunk of bread, two pickled onions the size of golf balls and an ample smothering of pickle. Leif looked approvingly at the feast before him.

'Hope you enjoy it,' said the blonde with a smile that stretched from cheek to cheek.

Leif grinned. 'I will.'

The blonde pouted her lips at him and winked. Leif took a sip of cider and watched her with a smile as she returned to the kitchen. She wasn't half bad. And her feast was even better. He set to with the appetite of a ravenous wolf.

'Then there's trips to the other islands,' continued the publican. 'You can get a boat to Winderley and Bolt. Mind you, there's nothing at Bolt. Just birds and a few ruins.

But if you fancy a trip one of the boatmen will take you.'

The publican reached under the bar and retrieved a grubby and well-worn guide which he passed to Leif. 'All the details are in there,' he said.

Leif glanced at the guide. It was titled *Excursions round Scurra*. On the front was a photo of a seagull perched on a groyne with a deserted beach in the background.

Leif propped the guide in front of him and began the task of separating the leaves of his lettuce.

The old woman coughed, picked up her bag and made her way slowly to the door.

'Goodnight, Ma,' Mainwaring called. 'Thank you.'

Ma paused, her eyes fixing on Leif for one last moment. She turned back to the door and made her way out, a stale smell following her. Mainwaring reached for an aerosol, went over to where she had been sitting, picked up the tankard and crisp packet and sprayed the area with a lavender scent, guaranteed by the makers to 'conquer unpleasant smells'.

'Sad case,' he muttered returning to the bar. 'Seventy years old and never been off Scurra. And you saw that bag? Carries all her valuables, such as they are, in that. I've seen some jewellery in there and money. Not a lot, but even so. I've told her, everyone's told her, it's not safe, but no she won't listen. Takes it everywhere she does. One day she'll get robbed.' The publican finished his pint. 'She has a home near Lower Arch, but she's hardly ever there. More often than not she sleeps rough. And,' Mainwaring leant closer to Leif. 'some say she sleeps among the Seven Stones.'

'Seven Stones?'

'An ancient circle. Some say there's magic in them stones. Fertility, ancient wisdom, all that sort of thing.' Mainwaring smiled and ran his hand through his hair. 'Don't believe it myself, but there's many that do.'

Leif unfolded the map that came with the guide.

'Where are these stones?' he asked.

'Around here.' Mainwaring vaguely pointed to an area near the centre of the island. 'There's a path to them from Lower Arch.'

'I might take a look,' said Leif.

'There's a stone in the middle of the circle,' added the publican. 'According to Ma that's the special one.'

'She knows all about them, then?'

'All there is to know. What's more, there's some that say she's a witch. Or, what do they call them?'

'Psychic?'

Mainwaring nodded. 'That's it, psychic. Many a time she's foretold things. Take Andy Thompson,' he continued. 'Ma told me she saw him silhouetted in black. Death 'ung on his shoulders, were her words, although she didn't tell Andy direct, of course. Just me and Jane. Two days later, what happens? His mum is knocked down by a dustcart of all things.' The barman shook his head. 'And that's not the only time. She saw McGuire's farm burn down. I 'eard her say it the day before it happened. *Smoke will rise in McGuire's*, she said, and she was right. The next day McGuire's farm went up. Though some mean folk wonder if she didn't start it herself.'

'Can she tell me the results of my finals?' asked Leif with a smile.

Martin Mainwaring looked thoughtfully at Leif. 'I dunno,' he mused. 'But. . . she was looking at you in a mighty strange way. Never seen her stare at anyone like she stared at you. Mighty strange it was. Mighty strange.'

Leif shook his head, half amused at all these typical folk tales of witches, omens and heaven knows what. It was all old stuff spun to entertain the visitors. But all the same, she *had* looked at him in a peculiar manner. Old women were fanciful and that one had looked quite batty, poor old thing. He turned his mind and enjoyment back to the devouring of his supper.

6

After coffee and some mints Juliet Tyler wandered through to the lounge of the Scurra Manor Hotel. It was a large room, illuminated by three ornate chandeliers with plush red velvet curtains at the far end of the room. The coffee tables contained the latest editions of glossy country magazines and she flipped through one or two idly. Two large mahogany bookcases bulging with ancient tomes stood at the near end of the room, but it was the pictures that most caught Juliet's eye. On one side of the room were some photographs of Scurra, on the other some paintings. The centrepiece was a large oil painting over the mantlepiece. Attached to the gilt frame was a label:

The Scurra Rock
by John Steelgate 1802-1871

The painting was of the towering cragged rock situated off the south-west coast. Gulls were perched at all levels or shown swooping down on the shimmering water. It was a majestic and timeless painting.

On either side hung two smaller works by Steelgate. One was of a family painted in 1829. There was the father, a proud sombre figure with a bushy beard and pointed side whiskers; next to him sat his wife, a meek mouse of a woman with a woeful expression. Beside them stood their children, a robust but studious-looking boy by his father and a smartly dressed young woman by her mother. She had long trailing hair and, unlike the others in the family, there was a hint of a smile on her unblemished face.

The third Steelgate painting was of a schooner moored against a cobbled wall in Narraport harbour.

In addition to the paintings, there were some prints of Scurra and some rural scenes by Pyne.

'Glad you're enjoying yourself.'

Juliet turned. Her father smiled fondly at her. 'It's good to see.' He gazed up at the print his daughter was admiring. 'What do you think?'

'I wish I could paint like that,' she replied wistfully. 'Pyne had such technique.'

'I think you *can* paint like that.'

Juliet smiled and shook her head.

'It's the technique. The nuances. The gestures. The character.'

'It will come,' said Sir Alec. 'Work and it will come.'

Juliet nodded. She had heard him say that many times. It was so much a part of his philosophy.

She turned and faced him. 'Dad,' she began. 'Where's Edward?'

'Talking to Strevans.'

'Why did you ask him to come on this holiday? We've gone on our own to places before.'

Sir Alec pursed his lips, a habit of his as he picked his words. 'He's a good golfing partner. And the doctors have told me I need the exercise.'

Juliet smiled and shook her head. 'That's not the reason.'

'He's an excellent adviser.'

'Dad,' persisted Juliet. 'The real reason.'

'You have it, my dear.'

'Dad,' said Juliet firmly. 'Edward can look after your interests in London without coming all the way to Scurra.'

'But he can't play golf if he's there, can he?'

'Dad, if you think you can bring Edward and me together you are mistaken. Edward might be a close associate of yours and a great golfing partner, but I don't like him.'

Sir Alec gazed at his daughter. She was so like her mother. Petite, long hair and with a glowing and freckled complexion. He smiled. 'I'm not asking you to like Edward. But I would like you to get to know him. You will need him when I'm gone.'

'Dad!' she protested.

'You have to face reality,' added Sir Alec. 'Last year I had that coronary. I can't go on forever.'

'But . . .' Juliet hesitated, looking back at the Pyne print as if to seek inspiration. 'Look, Dad, you're better now. You took the doctor's advice. You're almost back to your old self.'

'Almost,' said Sir Alec. 'But that doesn't alter the fact that you'll need someone to help you when I'm gone. Even if it's just with the business interests and your inheritance. And I want that person to be Edward. He knows the business so well, he's helped me manage it all for many years and I totally trust him. He's a good man, Juliet, and I know he cares a lot about you.' Sir Alec paused. 'Tomorrow morning I'm playing golf with Edward. In the afternoon I would like Edward to take you around Scurra. Just a drive.' Sir Alec paused, and added softly. 'For me, Juliet. Please.'

Juliet sighed. 'Dad, it's no use. Edward and I just do not get on.'

'Please, Juliet,' persisted Sir Alec. 'It's important.'

Juliet turned back to her father. He was looking at her pleadingly. And with a sigh, she relented. She came over and kissed his cheek.

'Well, just this once,' she said. 'You understand? After this, no more.'

Sir Alec nodded and patted Juliet gently on the shoulder.

'Good lass,' he said. 'Good lass.'

Juliet slipped into bed. It felt soft and comforting after such a long day. The first day of any holiday, with all the travelling and change was, in Juliet's view, always the worst. She wrapped the duvet tightly around her and closed her eyes. The clock on St Michael's church chimed eleven. Juliet heard only six of the chimes. Sleep came quickly.

The creaks started quite suddenly. At first Juliet dismissed them, turning in her bed and groaning. But the creaks persisted. Long sluggish creaks, as if someone was creeping on warped floorboards.

Juliet turned once more and glanced at the numbers on her bedside clock. 2.30. It was still dark. She closed her eyes and buried herself further in her duvet.

Creaks in an old building – it was quite normal.

Outside an owl hooted – then, another creak. This time quite close, as if someone was approaching her bed. Juliet opened her eyes, sat up and looked round warily. But despite the noise she could see no movement. Everything was still, just as it should be.

Juliet wondered if it was a pipe under the floor. Perhaps air in one of the pipes. She would mention it tomorrow and hope they could sort it out.

As the church clock chimed three, the creaks stopped, almost as suddenly as they started. And Juliet went back to sleep, unaware that another petal from one of the roses was fluttering down to the floor.

7

As Leif strode past the Bush Retreat, Rose Bush gave a cheery wave.

'Going to be a nice day,' she called. 'Good walking weather.'

Leif readily agreed and continued down the unmade road. He had decided to spend the morning exploring the immediate vicinity and go for a longer walk in the afternoon. Pear Beach, the beach where he had such fond memories, would be for another day. But first he needed to stock up on provisions.

The nearest shop was situated just beyond the Compass and was an old building, probably as old as the pub. The brick walls had been painted white and the window boxes overflowed with trailing lobelia. It would have been a pleasing sight had it not been for the posters and labels stuck haphazardly across the windows. Special offers, new products and an ageing poster advertising last year's pantomime.

The antique bell on the door spluttered as he entered. An elderly unshaven man in a crumpled shirt stood behind the counter and glowered at Leif.

Leif nodded at the shopkeeper and went straight to the rack of postcards hanging on one of the side walls. There were the usual seaside scenes of crowded and picturesque beaches, some thatched villages as well as some more risqué postcards. However, it was the engravings and photographs that caught his eye and it was one of these he selected for his mother. She was into nostalgia and would appreciate a sepia photo of Edwardian trippers heading towards Scurra on a paddle-boat.

Leif put the postcard on the counter. The old man picked it up and slipped the card in a brown paper bag.

'Stamps?' he grunted.

'No. But I'll have two cans of spaghetti,' said Leif.

The old man turned to the laden shelves behind him and reached up for the spaghetti, his shirt becoming untucked in the process. He put the cans on the counter and Leif glanced at the sell-by date. In a store like this it was wise to check. He asked for a few more things, selected some apples and took a yoghurt from the cool cabinet.

The bell on the door gave its half-hearted ring as another customer entered.

'Have you a large bag or box?' asked Leif.

The old man looked dubious. Paper bags for postcards was one thing, carrier bags or boxes another.

'Let's see,' he grunted. Placing his hand on his stomach, he bent down and reached under the counter.

'Will this do you?'

He thrust a cardboard box at Leif. It had once, a long time ago, contained four dozen packets of crisps. Now it contained a dead spider.

'That'll be fine,' declared Leif, tipping the remains of the spider on the floor before putting his purchases carefully in the box.

'Hallo.'

Leif turned, surprised at the friendly female voice and wondering who the speaker was addressing. Before him stood a smart young woman in a blue and white cotton dress.

'I thought it was you,' she continued. 'You were on the ferry. I recognised your beard.'

Leif nodded, suddenly recalling the moment he lay sleeping on the ferry floor, his wallet dangerously perched in the folds of his jacket.

'That's me,' he said, a wide grin appearing on his face. 'And I don't think I really thanked you for telling me about my wallet. It would have ruined my holiday if I'd lost it.'

'It was the least I could do.' The young woman hesitated. 'Are you staying locally?'

'At the campsite.' Leif nodded towards the box. 'Stocking up on provisions.'

She smiled. 'Well, have a nice holiday,' and she went over to open the door for Leif. Leif passed through, aware that the box was already buckling under the weight of his shopping.

The box lasted four minutes before one of the bottom flaps gave way and the cans of spaghetti rolled in the road. Leif retrieved them, put them back in the box and turned it on its side. He was just inspecting the loose flap when an emerald Rolls pulled up with the young woman at the wheel.

'Can I give you a lift?' she asked, adding with a broad smile, 'His boxes are about as good as his shop.'

'Oh, it's all right,' Leif replied. 'I'll manage. Somehow.'

The young woman watched as Leif carefully lifted the box, wrapped his arms round the broken base and pressed the top of the box against his chest. He went a few paces when an apple rolled out and landed in the ditch.

Leif looked across at the woman in the car. She was still watching him, much amused. She reached over and opened the passenger door. He grinned and walked across to the car, put the box on the floor and got in beside her. She slipped the car into gear and started off.

'This is a lovely car,' Leif said admiringly.

'It's my father's,' she replied. 'I've nothing so grand.'

'It's a lot better than my transport back home!'

The woman looked across at Leif. 'Oh, what have you got?'

'A bicycle with a puncture.'

She laughed. Her laugh was pleasing and musical

like her voice.

There was a 40-mph speed limit on Scurra and she drove the car slowly and effortlessly. The whole pace of life on Scurra was so much slower than on the mainland.

'You can drop me anywhere,' said Leif. 'It's not far now.'

She pointed to the unmade road. 'You're camping down there, aren't you?'

Leif nodded.

'I thought so. You can just see the top of one of the caravans from my window.'

The young woman slowed the car right down and Leif was just about to reach down for his box when she swung the car down the unmade road.

'You don't want to go down here,' Leif protested. 'It's a terrible road. Craters everywhere.'

'That's all right. I'm here to explore Scurra, so I might as well see this part.'

The unmade road petered out by the Bush Retreat giving way to a bumpy track used by the caravans and trailers. The woman stopped the car outside the house.

'Thanks,' said Leif.

She reached over to the back seat. As she stretched and turned her dress lifted a few inches above her knees and Leif tried not to look. He was all too aware of her beauty.

'Here,' she said, and she passed him an empty Marks and Spencer carrier bag. 'Use this.'

'Thanks.' Leif transferred the shopping from the box to the bag. He opened the passenger door, got out and reached for the bag and battered box. 'And thanks for the lift.'

She smiled. 'A pleasure.'

Leif took one more look at the young woman before closing the door. She was nice. Really nice. A warm, spontaneous person. He watched as she performed an effortless three point turn before heading back down the unmade road.

When the car was out of sight, Leif turned and was about to make his way back to his tent when he noticed Rose and Billy Bush staring at him from the kitchen window. He stopped and gave a little wave, but they did not respond. It was then that he noticed someone standing behind them, a dark and shadowy figure who now moved forward a little. The figure of an old woman – the same woman called Ma who had stared so menacingly at him at the pub.

8

Katherine Strevans stormed into the small office behind the reception desk. 'What's this I hear?' she demanded.

Norman, who was leafing through the *Sunday Times* magazine, glanced up. 'About what?' he enquired.

'Juliet Tyler. She has complained of noisy pipes.'

'I know.'

'Well, what have you done about it?'

Norman leant back in his swivel chair, resting his hands behind his head.

'I've had a word with Joe Sky.'

'And?'

'He won't come.'

'Have you tried anyone else?'

'Archie is coming. He said about three.'

Katherine looked hard at her husband. 'I don't like it,' she declared. 'It's always that room. And it hasn't happened for so long.'

Norman nodded. 'Let's hope it's a one off. Maybe it was the pipes, an airlock or something.'

'I wish it were.' Katherine hesitated a moment. 'But it would happen now. And to the Tylers of all people.'

'She was quite decent about it,' murmured Norman. 'Just asked if someone could take a look.'

'Yes, but what if Archie can't find anything? Can't fix it? If the noise gets worse? If . . . if anything else happens? What then?'

'We'll come to that at the time. Anyway, I'm sure Archie will come up with something. He usually does.'

Edward Harrison cast a disapproving glance at the Rolls.

'Wherever did you take it?' he demanded. 'It's all

splattered with mud.'

'It's the country roads,' replied Juliet. 'They're bad, especially after yesterday's rain.'

Edward grunted, unlocked the car and they both got in. He smiled at Juliet as she secured her seat belt. She looked attractive – very attractive.

Edward took the road through Lower Arch, noticing an antique shop as he drove through the village. There was a sign outside: FINE COLLECTION OF ANTIQUARIAN BOOKS FOR SALE. He was tempted to stop – antiquarian books were a passion of his – but he decided his visit would have to wait. On this occasion, Juliet came first. My God, this was his chance; he had to keep his mind on it.

His game that morning had gone well although he felt there was something in Sir Alec's manner that was detached, almost as if the old man was coming to terms with his own mortality. Sir Alec had always been a brave man and often spoken of his impoverish start in London with a father who, like that of Dickens, had got the family into debt. Entering the army, the young Alec had distinguished himself, won medals and risen high in rank before leaving to enter the world of commerce. Despite his amazing luck that led everyone to feel he must have some sort of magical charm or a special god on his side, he had never used his success in business merely to his own advantage. In fact, he was, in Edward's eyes, too philanthropic.

'I'm heaping up good Karma,' he used to say with a smile. 'Don't you think so Edward?'

Heaping up debts more like, was Edward's opinion and he had occasionally siphoned off some of the allotted charity money or directed it towards some 'charities' of his own making. At this rate there'd be little inheritance for his beloved daughter to enjoy. And sweet and simple of taste as she was, Juliet had always lived a life of ease and comfort. He was sure that she would never take kindly to anything less. What girl would? And he was more certain than ever that Sir Alec viewed him as his future son-in-law.

Edward Harrison glanced at Juliet. She was just gazing out of the window, at the rolling Scurra countryside.

'Do you prefer the beach or the downs?' he asked.

'The downs. I love hill walking.'

At the next village Edward took a single-track road to Baker's Cross, then over a cattle grid and up the steep ascent of Westcott Down. It was a twisty road and one popular with walkers. Several times Edward had to slow down as ramblers and families moved out of the way to let them pass. A toddler, hot and tired, bawled at his parents and would not get out of the way. Edward stopped and waited for a despairing father to pick the child up. The child squealed and struggled even more.

'Poor kid,' sympathised Juliet. 'I think it's had enough.'

Edward muttered something under his breath and edged the car past the struggling family.

He pulled up at the second viewpoint. There were no other cars there. And before them stretched Scurra: its lush fields, the farms, scattered communities and beyond, the shimmering sea, just as Steelgate had painted it over a hundred years ago.

'Fancy a walk?' asked Edward.

Juliet nodded.

They got out of the car, walked to the edge of the viewpoint and gazed out to sea.

'Ever done any sailing?'

Juliet shook her head.

'You should. It's exhilarating.' Edward paused. 'I'll arrange it sometime. I'll hire a boat and take you out.'

Juliet ignored his suggestion and started towards a path that led from the viewpoint to a plinth higher up on the down.

'I'm going to look up there,' she said.

The path was lined with heather and bracken and there was much evidence of rabbits. She hoped Edward would not be keen to walk such a path – especially in his highly glossed shoes – and be content to stay behind in the car, smoking. He could hardly complain if she took off. This was the countryside. This was Scurra, an island to explore.

But to her annoyance Edward followed her.

The plinth had a round metal plaque set in the top, indicating the direction and distance of certain features and towns. Although only slightly higher than the viewpoint where they had parked, it was now possible to see Gibbet Hill, the campsite below it and a blue tent pitched in the field below. Juliet wondered if it belonged to the young man she'd given a lift to. They could see the majestic white walled Scurra Manor Hotel and she could even make out the roof of Scurra General Stores.

Edward put his arm around Juliet. For a moment she froze before shrugging him off. She knew she had to get it over with.

'I'm sorry, Edward,' she said. 'But no. No flirting.'

Edward looked enquiringly at Juliet. 'I don't understand.'

'Yes, you do,' replied Juliet firmly. 'If you think our being together on Scurra will lead to romance, you're very much mistaken.'

'But Juliet, whoever said anything about romance? All I asked was for you to come out this afternoon. That's all.'

'And it's going to be all,' said Juliet. 'Just this one trip out and nothing more.'

'We'll see.'

'No, we won't see,' said Juliet firmly. 'Look, Edward, we are two different people. Our interests are completely different. We just don't have anything in common.'

'But—'

'We just don't, Edward. And if my father has this crazy notion of his trusted partner marrying his only daughter, he is totally and utterly mistaken.'

Edward took a deep breath and looked over at another part of Scurra, the part where the more popular beaches were concentrated. 'Well,' he said finally, 'that's me told, I guess. We might as well make the best of the afternoon. Let's have some tea at some olde-worlde teashop?'

Juliet nodded, and they made their way back to the car. Edward put the key in the ignition and glanced across at her. She was so stunning with her trailing black hair and delicate complexion. He reached over and kissed her. Lightly at first and then he pressed harder against her lips, feeling her breath in his mouth. She tried to push him away, but he resisted. He wanted to caress her. To love her. However, he pulled back. This was not the right time, not yet. Looking into her anxious and indignant hazel eyes, he smiled.

'That wasn't so bad, was it?' he asked.

'Yes, it was!' said Juliet and firmly slapped Edward round the face.

Recovering easily, he laughed, seized her hand in his and clutched it so tightly she felt he might break her fingers.

'I like spirit in a girl,' he murmured, 'makes the chase so much more exciting. I don't give up that easily, dear Juliet. Surely you know that by now?'

'Let my hand go,' she demanded, 'and take me back.'

'Whatever you say, madam.' He chuckled again, started the car and roared off towards the hotel. Juliet sank back in her seat and stared at the road ahead. She had a sudden sense of fear, not a sensation she was used to at all.

She would have to talk to Dad about Edward's behaviour. He was a bully and conniving bastard.

9

Leif returned to the campsite for a snack and to write the postcard to his mother before setting out once more for another, longer walk. As he passed the Bush Retreat, Rose Bush dropped the soggy pair of jeans she was about to hang out and rushed over to him.

'Mighty fine car you got a lift in,' she started, recalling the Rolls she had seen Leif get out of that morning.

'Was rather.'

'And a fine woman,' commented Rose. 'Her dad's worth a fortune.'

'You know who she is?'

'Oh yes,' replied Rose enthusiastically. 'Juliet Tyler, the daughter of Sir Alec Tyler. Worth a fortune he is.' Rose paused, taking delight in passing on the information. It had never occurred to her that Leif did not know who the girl was.

'She's staying up at Manor Hotel,' she continued. 'In the Dickens Suite, no less. Ann Walker, she's one of the cleaners, she told me. She said the Strevans, who own the hotel, had the suite all refitted for them. I mean it's not often they have the likes of the Tylers staying there.'

Rose Bush moved closer to Leif and whispered. 'And Sir Alec's not in the best of health. Charming he is, a real gentleman, but he's not well. The ticker, you know.' Rose said, patting her chest. 'And if anything happens to him, his fortune passes to his daughter.'

Leif nodded, content to know now who Juliet was. He had assumed she had come from a monied family but never as monied as the Tylers. And he was a tinge disappointed. Being a Tyler put her beyond his reach. With her wealth and background, she would never fall for an impoverished ex-student.

Leif was just about to continue on his way when he hesitated a moment and turned back to Rose.

'This morning,' he began. 'When I got out of the car, I saw you and Billy looking out of the window.'

'That's right,' agreed Rose, unbothered. 'I mean it's not every day we get a car like that pulling up outside our door.'

'But there was someone with you,' he added. 'An old woman. I saw her standing behind you. Was it Ma?'

'Ma?' Rose looked suspiciously at Leif. 'Ma?' she repeated. 'Who's Ma?'

'An old lady who lives round these parts. And I'm sure I saw her in your kitchen this morning.'

Rose shook her head vigorously. And Leif, who knew something about body language, knew she was lying.

'Oh well,' he said at last. 'Just thought I saw her, that's all.' And with a nod of his head, he turned and made his way down the unmade road, puzzled by Rose's reaction.

He went via the Scurra General Stores and saw the apple he had dropped still lying in the ditch. He posted his card to his mother and continued along the road until he came to Lower Arch. It was a sleepy village and, apart from an antique shop specialising in prints and antiquarian books, had little to offer the visitor.

Leif took a path that ran between two bordered cottages and overgrown gardens before coming out to a recreation area. Here the path split in two, in one direction leading to an aged hut belonging to Lower Arch football club and their uneven football pitch, the other way to the Seven Stones. This path was well defined and after running alongside an open field – popular with dog walkers – and crossing two stiles, it ran alongside a stream. The water was clear and sparkled as it rippled over the small rocks and stones. At one point, Leif bent down and sloshed some water over his face. It was cool and refreshing, particularly in the heat of the day.

The path and stream followed the same course for half a mile before parting, the stream continuing to cut its way through the fields while the path turned sharply right and up a steep incline to the Seven Stones. The stones were situated on a plateau, six being in a crude circle while the seventh, larger than the rest, was in the centre. The stones were of a hard sandstone, pale grey and resembling chunky headstones. Leif had hoped there might have been an information board giving the history of this ancient site but all he found was a small metal sign stuck in the ground: THE SEVEN STONES. ANCIENT MONUMENT.

Leif went up to one of the outer stones and placed his hands on top of one. It felt cold and curiously damp, even though the stone itself was perfectly dry and stood in the full light of the sun.

As he stood there, hands still on the stone, Leif surveyed the sight. It was so exposed, so ancient; the site of ceremonies, of worship and no doubt of sacrifice. The islanders would have spoken to their gods, have prayed and buried their dead. And now, so long after, these Seven Stones were all that remained, a testament to long forgotten generations.

Leif began to walk around them, absorbing the peace and mystery of the site. And from the plateau he could observe the surrounding downs and Gibbet Hill, with the gibbet clearly visible.

Leif noticed a robin perch on one of the stones and reached for his pocket camera. As he did so he noticed a well-worn carrier bag propped against one of the outer stones. It was the same one he had seen Ma carry around with her.

Forgetting the robin and photograph, Leif cautiously approached the bag. It was bulging with all manner of things. He could see a small wooden box pressed against one of the sides of the bag and a corner of a hard-covered book sticking through a tear in the plastic. Over the top of the bag was draped a dirty green pullover.

Leif turned around. He knew Ma was about. Somewhere she was watching him, her dark stony eyes staring at him, just as she had done at the Compass.

'Ma?' Leif called. 'Ma?'

The robin flew off. Everywhere was still. Leif was sure she was not behind any of the stones. They were too small. But she lurked somewhere, that he was certain.

Her bag lay by his feet and he wondered why she had left it. Perhaps he had startled her? And yet he had not seen anyone when he had arrived.

Leif glanced down at the bag once more, half tempted to rummage through it and find out more about this strange woman. But he left it where it was and made his way to the seventh and tallest of the stones, the one that stood in the centre.

It was weathered and rounded but it still stood proud; the heart of the monument.

Leif gazed at the stone, its secrets lost in its ancient walls. Lightly he touched the stone. Like the other it felt cold, very cold, and damp. And even though it, too, basked in the full sun it felt as if it had never known warmth and belonged to another age.

Leif shivered and began to make his way back to the outer circle, still aware of the carrier bag resting against one of the stones. He had almost reached the outer circle when a piercing screech rang out. Whether it was a bird, an animal or human, he did not know but it seemed to come from the centre of the circle. Startled, Leif spun round and, as he did so, his foot plunged into a rabbit hole and he tumbled forward. As he fell he caught a fleeting glimpse of Gibbet Hill. . . and of something hanging from the gibbet.

Leif shook himself, opened his eyes and stared back at the gibbet.

There was nothing there, nothing but the gibbet. And yet for a moment he had seen something. What, he was not sure – but something had been suspended there.

Leif struggled to his feet, brushed himself down and wriggled his foot. Apart from a slight graze, he had escaped unhurt. Carefully he continued to the outer stones, still puzzled by the screech and by what he had seen on the gibbet. And as he made his way from the site he noticed that Ma's carrier bag was no longer there.

10

Archie Cann slouched into the public bar of the Compass. Jane, the peroxide blonde, winked as he entered. She winked at most men, a habit she had acquired from her elder sister as a teenager.

'Pint of the usual, love,' grunted Archie, easing himself on a barstool.

Jane reached for Archie's tankard and pulled him a pint of bitter.

Martin Mainwaring sauntered through from the kitchen and joined Jane behind the bar.

'Been working today?' he asked, replenishing his own tankard.

Archie nodded. 'Up at the Manor.'

'And what do they want?' asked the publican.

'One of them guests complained of noisy pipes. Couldn't find nowt, though.'

Jane looked enquiringly at the odd job man.

'It wasn't in that posh suite they've got, was it?'

Archie nodded.

'Joe Sky won't go in it. Says there's summat strange about it. Summat . . .' Jane hesitated, '. . . unnatural. Yeah, that's the word he used, unnatural.'

'Yeah, well,' said Archie. 'That's Joe. Always thinking there's something strange in old buildings.'

'But he said there *was* summat strange at the Manor. I remember him saying so, but he never said what.' Jane paused. 'He hasn't told you, has he?'

Archie shook his head. 'Never said a word. 'Cept he wouldn't go near the place again.'

'Strange,' said Jane thoughtfully, ''cause Joe's not one to make things up. I wonder what he found?'

'All I can say,' said Archie, now beginning to wish

he had never mentioned the hotel, 'is that I found nowt odd.'

'Wasn't there a murder there once?' Jane asked, pulling another pint of bitter. 'Many years ago?'

Archie shrugged his shoulders.

'I'm sure there was,' continued Jane. 'Real gory, it was. Some stabbing. And they hung the person what did it.'

'Must have been a long time ago,' added Mainwaring.

'It was. My grandma told me. She told me all about local history, 'specially the bloodthirsty bits. And I'm sure she mentioned there was a murder there. A real scandal at the time and it was done by someone well-to-do.' Jane smiled. 'And they all turned out to see the hanging. Gory lot.'

'Don't know nowt about that,' said Archie.

'I'm sure it was at the hotel,' continued Jane. 'But it's changed its name since then.' Jane looked over at Archie. 'I wonder if it were bloodstains Joe saw?'

'Bloodstains?' retorted Mainwaring.

'Yeah. I mean Joe was replacing some floorboards, wasn't he? There could have been bloodstains on the floor. Even after all this time.'

'Well I don't know,' said Archie. 'All I know is that Joe won't go near the place. "Never," he said, "never." And Joe means what he says.'

Norman Strevans was sampling the Black Forest gateau when his wife breezed into the kitchen. She ignored Norman a moment and went straight to the head chef.

'Excellent meal, Paul,' she declared. 'Sir Alec sends his compliments.'

Paul nodded appreciatively. He had tried hard and it was good to have his efforts recognised, especially by one so distinguished as Sir Alec Tyler.

'Norman,' said Katherine now turning towards her

husband. 'I was wondering where you were.'

Norman licked the remains of the gateau from his fingers and smiled at his wife. He knew the smile would not do much, but it might help. She looked fidgety.

'Delicious cake,' he said. 'Everything all right, dear?'

'Yes,' said Katherine sharply. 'But you should be upstairs. The Tylers have almost finished.'

'We do have other guests apart from the Tylers,' Norman observed.

'Even so, I think you should be upstairs. And,' added Katherine, just catching her husband before he went, 'were there any messages while I was out?'

Norman thought back to the rather quiet afternoon.

'Archie checked Miss Tyler's room. He found nothing.'

Katherine nodded. She was not sure whether that was good or bad, but at least she could inform Miss Tyler her room had been checked.

'There was a call from Mrs Bassett for you. She said she'd call back tomorrow. Oh,' Norman hesitated, 'and there was a rather strange call.'

'Strange? How do you mean?'

'Some old lady. Kept asking if this was the Scurra Manor Hotel.'

'Did she say anything else?'

Norman frowned. 'Well, she did, but goodness knows what she was saying. Sounded a bit off her rocker.'

'So, what did you do?'

'Put the phone down. I mean, the Lorimers were waiting to see me.'

'How very peculiar,' said Katherine slowly. 'I wonder who she was?'

'I did ask her that,' said Norman. 'She said she was Ma somebody or other. I couldn't quite catch the rest.'

'Ma!' exclaimed Katherine. 'Oh, glory be, not her!' And she gave Norman a worried look before rushing out of the kitchen.

11

Sir Alec Tyler settled back in the sofa, a copy of *The Old Curiosity Shop* on his lap and a medium sweet sherry balanced on the armrest. Juliet sat beside him writing postcards, while Edward Harrison was opposite reading. Being what was termed as a speed-reader, he managed to devour a book a day and while Sir Alec always felt the fellow had surely not had time to savour the book, Edward still had an impressive recall about what he had read.

Sir Alec liked the Scurra Manor Hotel. It was as he expected. Well-appointed and homely. The Strevans could learn a lot more about catering and were a long way from ever realising the full potential of the hotel, but that was not his concern. He had done enough already – his life had been spent turning visions into reality.

Sir Alec opened the book but did not read. He liked Dickens and the characters that meandered through the pages. In his life he had met many Micawbers, some Scrooges, an odd Uriah Heap and he himself had felt like Dickens. Just as John Dickens had told Charles that if he worked hard one day he might own the splendid Gad's Hill House, so his own father had told him he would, through effort, realise his dreams.

And he had. He could afford anything he wanted, and it had all been achieved through his own efforts. His one wish was that Peggy could have lived to share in his success. She, of all people, had faith in him. Despite those early hard times and years of constant struggle with her ill health, she had shared his vision and kept his dream alive. But then, on the brink of their success, her heart had at last given way. Death had come on so suddenly and had robbed him of the only woman, besides his daughter, that he loved in his life.

Sir Alec glanced over at Juliet. She was so like her

mother, both in looks, poise and talents. And he was proud of her. One day everything would pass to her. He hoped she would cope but along with the security and luxuries the inheritance would bring, there would be the pressures, decisions and responsibilities. He wanted Juliet to be free from all that. If only she would warm to Edward; that young man was clever and capable, he would take care of everything. But Juliet seemed to distance herself from him. He wondered how their outing had gone. Neither had mentioned it or exchanged many words since their return. In fact, things felt distinctly chilly. He hoped Edward hadn't messed things up. Modern men seemed to have no idea how to woo a girl.

Juliet finished off another postcard and reached over for her address book.

'Today's been a success,' declared Sir Alec at last. 'We should do the same tomorrow.'

Edward looked up from his book.

'Golf?' he enquired.

Sir Alec nodded. 'It's a fine course. Deceptive. Especially the sixth, but I like it,' he paused and looked across at Juliet. 'Superb views,' he continued. 'Downs and sea. And you can also see the smaller islands and outcrops.'

'And *L'Esprit*,' added Edward.

'What's *L'Esprit*?' asked Juliet.

'A wreck. In low tide you can see the hulk,' Edward paused. 'There's a picture of it in the dining room. It sunk on 3rd April 1937 with the loss of fifty-one lives.'

'Are you sure it was fifty-one?' queried Sir Alec, looking over the top of his half-moon glasses.

Edward chose not to rise to Sir Alec's bait. 'There are other wrecks visible, too,' he continued and glanced across at Juliet. 'If you are interested, I could take you to the Wreck Museum. I believe it contains some fine exhibits.'

'I'll think about it.'

'I'd like to see it,' said Sir Alec. 'We'll go tomorrow afternoon.'

Juliet shifted uneasily and looked across at her father.

'I was planning to go for a long walk and do some sketching,' she said. 'Explore the island.'

'There's plenty of time for that,' replied Sir Alec dismissively. 'This is only our second day.' Sir Alec reached for his sherry. 'So, it's decided then. Golf in the morning when Juliet can do her walking. And the Wreck Museum in the afternoon.'

'Sounds ideal,' said Edward and he smiled at Juliet.

Annoyed, Juliet ignored him and began another postcard.

An hour later Edward had finished his book, Sir Alec was immersed in *The Old Curiosity Shop* and Juliet, having completed her postcards and diary, was drawing in her sketch pad. At first, she just doodled. A round oval shape, then she added a goatee beard and two eyebrows. Next, she filled in the rest of the features, letting her imagination run away with her. A long, pointed nose, elf like ears, wide eyes and a mass of straggly hair.

Her father looked over at the drawing and smiled.

'Anyone in particular?'

Juliet shook her head.

'No. No one.' She looked at her doodle. It *was* no one – but for the goatee beard. That belonged to the man camped out in the field. The man she had met on the ferry. The pleasant young man she had seen at that appalling shop and given a lift to that morning. She hoped she would see him again.

'I think I'll go to bed,' Juliet said at last. She reached over and gave her father a kiss. He responded with a tired but content smile.

'Good night, dear.' And he too eased himself up, leaving Edward sitting in his chair lost in thought.

Juliet stood in her silk nightshirt looking out of her bedroom window. There was no one outside to see her. Apart from a few farms, much of Scurra was in darkness. She could just make out a small patch of white in one of the fields – the roof of one of the caravans at the campsite. And beyond that rose the dark mass of the downs.

Juliet drew the curtains and climbed into bed. It felt comfortable and relaxing. Scurra had been a strange choice for her father. These days he preferred the warmth and sunshine of the Caribbean. He had once mentioned that it held some special youthful memories for him and that he had always wanted to return some day. She was beginning to like the place and could see the attraction it held for him. Sir Alec had remarked last night that little had changed on the island. In some ways, it was as if time stood still over here. Quiet roads, unspoilt countryside and with so much at a slower pace. The brochures called Scurra 'The Relaxing Isle', and she thought it appropriate.

So tomorrow she would walk as far as she could and take her sketchbook and little box of paints with her. It would give her inspiration for when she got back to work. Maybe she'd go over the hills behind the campsite. And in the afternoon the wretched museum that Edward had mentioned. She did not want to go. It was just another excuse for her father to get her and Edward together again. Damn Edward. And he'd had the effrontery to kiss her. She should have pushed him away the moment he made his advance. Rejected him once and for all. It would not happen again. Never.

Slowly, thinking of Edward, her father, planning her walk, Juliet drifted off to sleep. And she slept deeply and soundly.

Outside all was quiet. Occasionally an owl hooted, and at half past one a dog gave chase to a terrified cat. The cat's meow pierced through the night before it managed to affect its escape up a tree. On the hour and half-hour, the clock on St Michael's chimed. A gentle breeze blew.

At two thirty-five Juliet woke with a start. From deep slumber she became instantly awake. Anxiously she looked round her darkened room. All was still. There was no noise, no creaking, no noisy pipes or squeaking floorboards. But something had woken her, that she was sure.

She eased herself up and looked at her bedside clock. She groaned, hoping it was almost morning.

Juliet slipped back under the duvet and closed her eyes. She lay motionless, wishing and willing for sleep to return.

But it did not.

Juliet adjusted her position and wrapped the duvet even tighter around her, annoyed with herself for having woken up for no apparent reason. She was usually such a sound sleeper.

It was some fifteen minutes later before her tiredness began to overtake her and once more she began to drift off. And, as she lay on the brink of sleep, a light tapping started at her window.

Slow, rhythmic, persistent.

Tap.

Tap.

TAP.

And the room began to chill.

12

The ancient bell above the door protested feebly as Leif entered the shop. The old shopkeeper glanced up. He was considerably smarter than the day before, in a crisp, white shirt, black tie and ironed trousers. He cast a sorrowful glance at Leif and mumbled something incoherent under his breath.

The young man went up to the counter and gave his order.

The shopkeeper took the small packet of digestive biscuits Leif wanted from the shelf behind him while Leif selected some provisions from the cool cabinet.

The door opened as another customer entered the shop. Leif turned, hoping it was Juliet, but instead it was an elderly but smart woman with her hair dyed a grey-blue. She went straight to the counter, ignoring Leif.

'I've just heard the news, Steve,' she said. 'I'm so terribly, terribly sorry.'

The old man's face crumpled as if in pain.

The lady turned to Leif, who was gathering up his shopping.

'It's Bill,' she said. 'He's dead.'

'I'm sorry,' said Leif softly, wondering who Bill was.

'Poor Steve,' she said, looking at the old fellow with sympathy. 'Shall I make you a cup of tea?'

Steve shook his head and sighed dismally.

The woman's bony fingers gripped Leif by his wrist. 'They were good friends,' she said earnestly. 'Inseparable they were. Steve and Bill.'

'Right.'

'Archie found him at the side of the road. Hit by a car, he was. Didn't stand a chance, not a chance.' The woman shook her head sadly. 'And the driver never stopped.' She paused and turned back to the old man. 'He was a lovely dog, was Bill. Really affectionate.'

Now that he understood, Leif felt compassion for the old man who had lost his companion.

'I know what it feels like,' he said, 'I was devastated when that happened to my dog when I was a kid.'

Steve made no reply but gave a little nod.

Leif left the shop. With his shopping secure in his small rucksack, he walked smartly up the road towards Lower Arch. Several cars passed him, but not the emerald Rolls.

Just past the antique shop, Leif took the path leading to Gibbet Hill. There were several approaches to the hill, including a steep path that led up from behind the campsite, but this was going to be a leisurely walk. An all-day walk. The weather was fine, and it was already warm.

The path was well-defined. Little wooden stakes daubed with yellow had been set out along the route, indicating it was one of the recommended walks on Scurra. The yellow walk led to the top of the down where the more energetic could pick up the red walk, a walk that led along the top of the downs before dropping down to Scurra point, not far from the lighthouse.

After just five minutes climbing, Leif had commanding views of the island. He could even see the plateau containing the Seven Stones and some children playing chase round the centre stone while their mother recorded their delight with a camcorder. He could see the campsite and scattered village of Lower Arch. Beyond were fields of grazing cattle and the rich farmland of Scurra.

Several times Leif stopped to admire the tiny flowers that grew on the downs or the birds that hovered overhead. The grass was soft and springy. It was pleasant walking and comfortable on the feet.

The clock on the church at Lower Arch struck ten, its distinctive *dong*ing echoing for miles around.

Halfway up the hill Leif stopped to take a photograph of the plateau and Seven Stones. The family had gone, and the stones stood straight and tall in the sunlight, as they had done for over two thousand years. They looked mystical, as if still radiating their own powerful aura.

He continued the climb. From further up he could make out golfers on a far distant course and could also see some of the many islands dotted around Scurra.

A tall man wearing nothing but shorts walked briskly down the path towards Leif, his muscular body glistening with sweat.

'*Pardon*,' said the man with a strong French accent. 'Lower Arch, this way?'

Leif nodded.

'Just keep going,' Leif told him, and the Frenchman continued on his way.

The gibbet was now clearly in sight. It was taller than Leif had thought, and it dominated the whole down. Leif stopped and looked at it for a moment. It was a grotesque reminder of the past. Many bodies had no doubt hung and rotted on the gibbet – the bodies of murderers, criminals, pirates and a few unfortunate innocents. And it stood as a monument to all.

Leif pressed on. Several other walkers, making their way from the top, passed him, each wishing him a good morning.

It was starting to get hot, the path steeper. Leif quickened his step and continued until he was at the top and standing by the large and menacing gibbet.

Leif eased his rucksack from off his shoulders, undid some of the buttons on his shirt and sat down, propping himself against the base of the wooden structure. He was hot but exhilarated. He took a can of Coke from his rucksack, pulled back the ring and drank, a cold dribble running onto his beard before dripping on his chest.

From where he sat he could see almost all the island. It was so peaceful and unspoilt and he quietly soaked up the beauty and tranquillity that lay before him.

'We meet again.'

Leif turned, recognising the voice immediately. It was Juliet Tyler and she was standing looking down at him.

'You seemed miles away,' she said smiling.

Leif began to ease himself up.

'No, don't get up,' said Juliet. 'I was just out for a walk.' She looked round. 'It's so beautiful up here, so fresh and clear.'

Leif got up.

'Which route did *you* take?' he asked.

Juliet was not as hot as he nor out of breath.

'The path behind the hotel. It wasn't too bad. Only took thirty minutes.'

'I came up from Lower Arch,' said Leif. 'Fancy a drink?' and he bent down and took out the other can of Coke from his rucksack.

'No,' said Juliet. 'You might need it later.'

'Go on,' insisted Leif.

Juliet hesitated before finally taking it. She opened the can and took some sips. 'From Scurra General Stores?' she enquired with a grin.

Leif nodded.

'And how was that dreadful man?'

Leif ran his hands through his thick fair hair.

'A bit upset,' he replied. 'His dog had just been run over.'

'Oh dear, poor fellow.' She looked genuinely sad. After a moment's pause, she turned to him and said, 'I don't know your name.'

'It's Leif.'

'That's unusual. Scandinavian?'

'My father was Danish. But I've lived in England all my life.' Leif paused. 'And I hear you are Juliet?'

Juliet shrugged and nodded, her eyes meeting Leif's. Then she looked down at the ground and Leif felt he shouldn't have come out with that.

'I'm sorry,' he whispered.

Juliet looked back at him, a bemused look on her face. 'Why?'

'I should have let you tell me yourself. It makes out I've been prying.'

'No, it doesn't.' Juliet laughed. 'I'm used to it. It comes from having a famous dad.'

Leif smiled too and watched her as she tilted her head back and drank some more from the can. She was so beautiful, so fresh and vital. She attracted him as no other woman had done before. She came from such a different world to his and yet it felt as if they had always known one another, as if she was a friend from a long time ago, an ordinary person like himself. There were no airs and graces, nor anything spoilt about her.

'I feel mean,' said Juliet, putting down the empty can. 'Now I've left you without a drink.'

'I'll get another,' said Leif. And together they stared out across the island, at the beauty all around, oblivious to the gibbet behind them.

'Are they the Seven Stones?' Juliet asked, pointing to the plateau.

Leif followed her gaze to the stones and nodded. All the stones were clearly visible and there was someone walking between them. Not a family this time. Just a single solitary figure. Slowly, hesitatingly making their way between the stones.

'I was thinking of walking there tomorrow,' said Juliet.

'They are quite interesting,' replied Leif, staring at the figure. 'Mystical.'

'You've been there?'

Leif looked back at Juliet and nodded.

'Yesterday,' he replied. 'It's a nice walk. Along by a stream and then a short climb to the plateau.'

Leif glanced back at the stones. There was now no one there. The figure had gone and yet just a moment ago he had seen it so clearly.

'Then I'll go there,' declared Juliet. 'Tomorrow.' She hesitated and looked back at Leif. 'Is anything wrong?'

'I don't know,' replied Leif thoughtfully. 'I mean, did you see someone walking down there just then?'

Juliet nodded. 'Yes. Yes, there was someone. Looked like an old woman.'

'Can you see her now?'

Juliet looked back, her eyes fixed on the ancient circle.

'No,' she said shaking her head.

'So at least I wasn't dreaming it.'

'Why should you be?'

'Because I thought for a moment I was seeing things.' Leif hesitated. 'It's very odd. We both saw that figure, right?'

Juliet nodded.

'Well, now it's gone, but where could it go? From here we look down on the main approaches to the plateau. But there's no one around.'

She looked down on the scene below and frowned. 'You're right. It's ... it's all a bit strange.'

Leif turned and looked at Juliet.

'Don't go to those stones. Not alone.'

Juliet, aware of Leif's increasing anxiety, looked startled.

'Because of that person?'

'Maybe, I don't know. But there is something down there. Something odd.'

Juliet thought for a moment. 'All right, you've convinced me,' she said. 'I won't go. Not alone.' And she glanced back at the gibbet. 'What with the weird noises in my room that make me feel as if I was at Wuthering Heights, and the person at the stones, the place is beginning to give me the creeps.'

'What sort of weird noises?'

Juliet looked into Leif's candid blue eyes. She felt he wasn't the sort of person to laugh at her as Edward and her father had done when she had told them. In fact, they had told her she'd been reading too many Gothic novels. All the same, in the light of day things always seemed so different. Maybe she *had* dreamt it all.

She smiled and shrugged, 'Oh, I think I had some sort of nightmare. I find it hard to sleep in a strange bed and these old hotels creak and groan so much,' Juliet paused. 'I take it nothing happened when you were at the stones?'

'I saw something,' he replied, like her about to dismiss his experience lightly, 'but . . . God!'

For a moment Leif saw himself back at the stones – hearing the screech, reliving the fall, seeing something hanging from the gibbet, something that he now realised was a body. He jumped up and stared at the tall menacing structure.

Juliet also rose in haste and stared up with him. She suddenly felt a sense of tremendous fear.

13

Two hours later Juliet stood looking out of her bedroom window and across the rolling fields of Hunter's Valley to the downs and the distant gibbet.

She had loved the walk. The exhilaration, the freedom and the beauty. And she had met Leif again. He was so startled – and pleased – when she had found him propped up against the base of the gibbet, almost as surprised as the time when she had told him he was about to lose his wallet.

Juliet felt deeply attracted to Leif. He was gentle and quiet; his mass of fair hair and goatee beard made him quite handsome. She liked scholarly men who took life with some seriousness. She realised he must be a little younger than her if he had just finished his first degree but that didn't matter. He struck her as far wiser and more sensible than Edward though definitely not so worldly . . . and that was also a good thing. She hoped her wealthy background wouldn't put him off getting to know her.

Then she thought of the stones, the figure they had both seen that had so mysteriously disappeared. And she recalled the sudden look of terror on Leif's face. He had tried to cover it up, but he was obviously worried. Something, she did not know what, had made him fearful but he had remained silent on the subject and tried to cover it up. She respected that but hoped he would trust her enough to tell her someday.

Her bedroom door opened. It was Edward. Pristine, pompous and immaculate in his white trousers and crisp open-necked blue shirt.

'Your father is waiting,' he announced and joined Juliet by the window. He smelt strongly of aftershave.

'Good view,' he said. 'If you like this sort of thing.'

Juliet felt Edward edge closer towards her. She

moved away, grabbed her handbag from her bed and headed for the door. Edward followed closely behind, watching her every move.

Leif finally came to Heaven's Drop, the part where the downs descended sharply to the beach and sea. It was precipitous and there were signs advising of an alternative but longer and less steep route.

He decided to go the direct way. The path was pitted with chalk and at several stages steps had been cut to make the path a little easier. Several energetic walkers ascending the path stood to one side to let him pass and catch their breath. Even for the energetic, the climb up Heaven's Drop was a stiff challenge.

Halfway down Leif perched himself on a rock. He reached for his rucksack to check there was nothing left from lunch. There was not. And no drink either. At the end of the path he would go to a cafe and treat himself to a tea. For the moment, he settled back to admire the views, watching the sea breaking over the many small rocks around the island and the dozen or so yachts with their blue, red, and yellow spinnakers. A water skier was struggling to remain upright as the speedboat pulling him steered a deliberately twisty course.

He could also see Scurra lighthouse. It was a magnificent tall building, almost all white and with its light and sirens ever at the ready. To the east was Pear Beach. It looked busy. He could make out the holiday makers basking on the sands and splashing in the sea and there was a cluster of children attentively watching a Punch and Judy show. Somewhere on that beach, many years ago, he had buried his father in the sand. When it was quieter, maybe early in the morning, or one evening, he would visit the beach and say a prayer to the memory of Peter Olsen. But not now, not when it was so busy.

After some moments Leif scrambled to his feet and continued to the bottom of the down, passing a family squabbling over a picnic while their son tried to extract a tangled kite from a bush. Crossing a stile, he headed a little way along the road towards an old stone building. Outside hung a sign, HEAVEN'S DROP TEA GARDENS, and underneath was suspended a smaller sign advertising FRESH SCURRA ICE CREAM.

Leif opened the gate at the side of the building and made his way round to the back garden. Red hot pokers, lupins and roses grew in profusion and on the newly cut lawn were five round white tables and several plastic chairs. One of the tables still had the debris of previous customers but otherwise the tea garden appeared deserted.

He slipped his rucksack off, put it on one of the chairs and knocked at the back door. As he did so, the door opened a little.

'Hold on a tic,' called a high-pitched voice. 'Just coming.'

Leif caught the smell of freshly baked bread.

He waited. And waited. Hanging just inside the door was a rack of postcards and a selection of small guides; *Walks on Scurra*, *Scurra Walks for Motorists*, *Myths and Folklore of Scurra* and *Murders of Scurra*. The last had an engraving of the gibbet on the cover and Leif eased it from the rack.

'Sorry to have kept you waiting,' said the tea shop owner, a large man with a mass of bleached curly hair and an earring dangling from his left ear. His apron was splattered with dough. 'Had to get the last lot in the oven,' he explained.

'Smells good,' said Leif with a smile. 'A pot of tea, please.'

'Earl Grey, English breakfast, Darjeeling, Kenyan, Assam, Ceylon or herbal? We do the full range, you know.'

Leif pursed his lips thoughtfully. He was no connoisseur of tea. 'I'll try the Assam,' he decided.

'Fine,' replied the man picking some dough off his hands. 'With you in just a mo'.'

Leif returned to one of the tables, taking the booklet with him. It was several years old and published by the Scurra Publishing Company. Inside the local author had dedicated the book to his many friends on Scurra, with kind acknowledgements to Archibald McGee, librarian and President of the Scurra Ghost Club, Edward Fitzroy, Trustee of the Local History Society and Ma Demuth.

That had to be weird old Ma! thought Leif. With her local knowledge and strange ways, it seemed almost inevitable she would be involved in a publication like this.

Leif flicked through the closely printed pages. There were grim tales of young men being hung for stealing hens and sheep; of Rob Cassels, a notorious pirate who was shot during a raid on Scurra and taken directly to the gallows and hung. There were further descriptions of the savagery inflicted on the body after the hanging, but Leif skipped a few pages on. There was a piece about a murder at Hunter's Lodge and the hanging of twenty-year-old Mary Hunter, convicted of stabbing one Walter Games. And there were other tales. Of a madman named Luke, who had terrorised the islanders and evaded capture for three years. When he was finally traced to a cave not far from Heaven's Drop, the remains of five adults and seven children were found.

'Nice day, isn't it?'

Leif looked up and the tea shop owner was heading towards him with a pot of tea, two wholemeal scones and a pot of strawberry jam and some cream.

'I just wanted the tea,' said Leif.

The owner looked pained.

'Oh, I'm so sorry. I just thought. . . well, everyone has cream tea here. It's tradition.'

Leif looked at the scone and felt the pangs of hunger arise.

'Trouble is, I didn't bring much money with me.' Leif reached in his pocket and took out the coins it contained.

'That'll more than cover it,' said the man taking some of the coins and the booklet. 'Fascinating,' he said glancing at the cover. 'There's more to Scurra than meets the eye. Strange goings-on.' The tea shop owner winked knowingly, turned and made his way back to the cottage. Moments later he reappeared with the few pence change.

'How do you mean, strange goings-on?' Leif asked.

The man looked quizzically at Leif and pulled on his earring.

'Well, it's history. It's old customs and . . . things that have happened. Still happen. There's . . .' The man suddenly stopped and turned his head sharply towards the door. 'Oh, glory be, that's the timer,' and he dashed back indoors.

Leif settled back to enjoy his cream tea. *This is the life*, he thought. Peace and contemplative quiet were what he enjoyed most in the world. He was a man who wanted little and could manage on less. Sometimes he wondered why he'd bothered about sweating so hard to get a degree. He could live simply and happily in a place like this if only there was work to be found. Maybe he could open his own tea shop. He watched as a robin hopped onto a nearby table and pecked at some crumbs left by a previous customer and fantasised serving at his own little cafe with Juliet assisting.

14

After dinner Juliet slipped on her pastel green jacket and picked up the bag containing the Scurra shortbread biscuits she had bought at the Wreck Museum.

Her father sat on the settee engrossed in a book. Edward was in his room.

'Just going for a walk,' she announced. Her father looked up briefly, smiled and continued reading.

It was a delightful evening. The air was cooler and preferable to the muggy heat of the afternoon. Several other guests staying at the hotel were also out walking and a Dutch couple, on honeymoon, smiled at her as she passed them.

Juliet walked with a spring in her step. She felt content, happy to be among the beauty and tranquillity of Scurra. The fields around were lush, the hedgerows were scented with yellow honeysuckle and dog roses and abundant with brambles whose white flowers were now turning to as yet unripe fruit.

A woman about Juliet's age cantered by on a horse. She inclined her head as she went; life was so much slower on Scurra than on the mainland and the people seemed friendlier. Just like Leif, she also wondered what it would be like to live on Scurra – to be free from the pace and demands of city life. It would be wonderful, and she could certainly afford to move. But she did so enjoy her work as an illustrator and, for the moment, she needed to be based in London. And she also needed to be near her father.

She preferred not to think about her father's condition, but she knew he was not the man he used to be. Somehow his zest had diminished, and it seemed as if he was gradually winding down and passing his concerns to Edward. Damn Edward. When she did inherit, she decided that Edward would have to go. She'd find a replacement she could trust.

A tractor's horn blasted out, making Juliet jump. The tractor driver, wearing a hat several sizes too big, gave Juliet a toothless grin. She hadn't seen the tractor about to turn out of the field and the driver found the whole incident highly amusing.

Quickening her step, she followed the road round a bend. A rabbit hopped out and looked at her before jumping back in the hedgerow. She heard laughter and giggles from the other side of the hedge and caught sight of a couple locked in a passionate embrace.

She continued up the road and as she walked a sense of unease began to creep over her. Although she could see no one she felt as if someone was watching, lurking unseen behind one of the hedgerows. Clutching the packet of shortbread, she broke into a trot. She wanted to get to the unmade road, to find Leif, to talk to someone she knew. For some reason Scurra suddenly seemed empty and she felt all alone.

And vulnerable.

Leif waited patiently outside the phone box while a teenager, one of many staying at the campsite, assured his mother he was all right, eating well and enjoying his time on Scurra. He omitted to mention the lurid details of an illicit drinking bout.

After further pleasantries and assurances, the lad put the phone down, retrieved the coins he had not used and left the box, holding the door open for Leif.

Leif dialled his home phone number. He had promised his mother he would phone to let her know how he was getting on. The phone rang but there was no response. Perhaps she was with David, the new man in her life. She seemed to be changing, going out more and, after so many years of loneliness, beginning to enjoy life again.

Leif put the receiver down and picked up the dog-eared telephone directory that lay in the booth. Out of curiosity he looked up Demuth. There was only one entry. James Demuth, Waverly, The Esplanade, Pear Beach. He wondered if he was in some way related to the mysterious Ma? Maybe.

Leif tried his home number once more. He let the phone ring many times before finally replacing the receiver.

On leaving the phone booth, he saw Billy Bush and a buxom girl waiting outside. Leif held the door open and the girl entered.

'Hallo, Billy.'

Billy looked at Leif and nodded in vague recognition.

Leif began to set off down the road.

'Someone's been looking for you,' muttered Billy.

Leif turned, puzzled. 'For me?'

Billy nodded. 'Some woman,' he replied, and then added with a smile. 'Bit of all right.'

'Where is she now?'

Billy shrugged his shoulders.

'When was this?'

''bout fifteen minutes ago.'

'Damn!' Leif had no doubt it was Juliet. He knew no one else on Scurra and it seemed he had missed her – all for a phone call he didn't even make. Quickly he ran back down the road until he got to the unmade road. There he paused, wondering which way to go. He desperately wanted to see Juliet. Fifteen minutes, Billy had said. That would be enough time for her to find his tent, discover he was not there and then begin to make her way back, assuming she was not in the car.

He decided to stick to the road and started to run in the direction of the hotel. He ran around a bend and saw a couple walking arm in arm.

'Excuse me,' he panted. 'Have you seen a woman walking this way?'

The man looked at Leif thoughtfully. 'Yeah,' he said. 'There was an old woman with a carrier bag. That one?'

'No!' said Leif, annoyed at the thought of Ma. 'A young woman.'

'Ah, we did see someone else,' replied the man. 'We've only just passed her. If you're quick, you'll catch her up.'

Leif started off once more, this time running even faster. He ran around another bend and saw the lone figure of Juliet walking ahead of him.

'Juliet!' he yelled. 'Juliet!'

Juliet turned and, as soon as she saw Leif, started back towards him. She smiled as they met but looked pale and a touch anxious.

'I've been looking for you,' she said.

'And me for you,' replied Leif. 'I was told there was someone looking for me and I guessed it was you.' Leif paused, his blue eyes looking intently at Juliet. 'Well, I hoped it was you,' he added softly.

Juliet smiled and looked pleased.

'Would you like to come back to the campsite?' he asked. 'I'll make you a cup of tea – my special brew.'

'I'd like that,' she said, and together they headed back.

'It's not exactly posh,' said Leif as they approached his tent.

'I think it's fine.'

'But compared to the hotel, I mean.'

'The hotel is not my choice,' Juliet declared. 'Besides, I think being camped out like this is lovely. All the fresh air, the beautiful surroundings. It's just so natural.'

'And cheap,' added Leif.

'Well yes, that's a useful factor. And there's that lovely lady at the campsite. She told me where you were camped.'

'You'll never guess her name.'

Juliet shook her head.

'Rose Bush.'

Juliet laughed. 'I once knew a Lavender Bush,' she said. 'Brilliant at Maths, she was. At most things really.' Juliet hesitated and handed Leif the bag she was carrying. 'This is for you.'

Leif took the packet. 'Whatever for?' he asked, a little bemused.

'It's to thank you for the Coke you gave me on the downs. I felt dreadful after.'

'It wasn't off, was it?'

'No!' laughed Juliet. 'Because I left you without a drink. And it turned out such a hot day.'

'But you shouldn't have. I got something at a tea garden. Cream tea, no less. Delicious, but not something I can afford every day! 'Leif opened up the bag and took out the shortbread. 'Thanks,' he said. 'I'll enjoy this.'

Leif unlocked the tent, pulled down the zip, took out his bag of provisions and retrieved the stove, saucepan and bottle of water tucked just inside the fly sheet. Juliet stood by and watched as Leif put the water on to boil.

'I think camping is great,' she declared. 'It's just so . . . so natural.'

'A bit rough and ready,' admitted Leif, pulling two sweatshirts out of the tent and spreading them on the grass. 'Sorry I haven't any chairs.'

'I'll sit on the grass,' Juliet said. She smiled at Leif and glanced down at one of the sweatshirts Leif had set out before her. 'What's *Leifu*?' she asked.

'Hmm?' queried Leif.

She pointed to the small notebook jutting out from

one of the folds of the sweatshirt. On the stiff blue cover was written in neat blue handwriting, *Leifu*.

'Oh, that,' he said dismissively. 'Something I've been working on.'

Juliet looked at him inquiringly.

'I might show you some time,' he added.

She pouted a little. 'Why not now?'

He grinned. ''Cause it's . . . well, it's private.'

'Give me a clue.'

Leif thought for a moment.

'Heard of *haiku*?'

'Some sort of Japanese poetry?'

He nodded. 'Well, it's my form of *haiku*.'

'That's interesting,' said Juliet thoughtfully. 'I'd like to hear some.'

'Some time,' said Leif, and he reached over and reduced the heat on the stove. He dropped a tea bag in each of the flask cups and poured in the hot water.

'I haven't any sugar,' he apologised.

'I don't take it.'

She watched him as he stirred in the powdered milk. 'Aren't you cold at night?' she asked, suddenly shivering as she became aware of the drop in temperature.

'Sometimes. But I've a good sleeping bag and thick jumpers.' Leif handed Juliet the cup of tea and watched as she raised it to her lips. It was not as hot as he would have liked.

'This is really lovely,' she murmured. 'You know, I really envy you out here. It's so quiet and still.'

Glancing round the field and finally up at Gibbet Hill, she turned back to look at Leif, her expression serious. 'So, what *was* it up there?'

He put his cup down and edged nearer to her. He gazed quickly into her hazel eyes then looked away over the fields. She was very wise, very mature, yet there was an air of vulnerability and unworldliness about her that made him hesitate.

'Please, what was it?' she insisted.

'How do you mean?' he hedged.

'When I saw you on the downs you came over. . . well, a bit strange. Almost as if you'd seen a ghost. I know you said it was nothing, but it *was* something. Wasn't it?'

Leif sighed. 'It was just a stupid thought.'

'What, Leif?'

He shifted uneasily. 'Well, if you really want to know, when I was at the Seven Stones I tripped in a rabbit hole. As I fell I thought I saw something hanging from the gibbet.' He paused then added, 'This morning, on the downs, I had a crazy notion of what I think I saw.'

'What?' She looked anxious and he lightened his tone of voice.

'A body.'

'Oh, my God!'

Leif gave a little laugh and a shrug. 'It's okay, it's okay! It must have been a trick of the light. When I looked back, it had gone.'

Her expression was dubious. They drank their tea in silence for a few moments then Leif said, 'Anyway, what about you?'

'Me?'

Leif nodded. 'Tonight, when we met, *you* looked worried. Why?'

Juliet put her cup down and ran her hand awkwardly through her thick black hair.

'That was crazy as well. It was nothing either.'

'Seems we both keep finding things we declare are nothing really. It's important you tell me,' he said, and gently laid his hand on her knee. Juliet looked at Leif's hand and rested her own on his.

'It was just before I met you tonight. I was walking

along the lane and it felt as if I was being watched. Then all of a sudden, this old woman appeared. She was a sort of tramp. Her face was wrinkled and dirty and she had piercing black eyes. She startled me and when she saw my reaction she started to laugh. It was horrid, Leif, really horrid.'

Turning his hand, Leif clasped Juliet's hand and held it tightly, raising it to his chest.

'That woman,' he said, 'seems to turn up everywhere! That's Ma Demuth.'

'You've seen her too, then?'

'So have you,' he replied. 'I'm sure it was her we saw at the Seven Stones this morning. You know, the person we saw one moment who'd gone the next.'

'Was she at the stones when you were there?'

'I think she was,' said Leif. 'And I think we should be careful of her. There's something weird about her. Something frightening.'

'But she's just an eccentric, Leif.'

'I know. But … but she keeps turning up, as if she is always there. Always watching. And there's some people here who reckon she's a witch.'

Juliet smiled and gently retrieved her hand from his clasp. It had felt comforting the way he had held her hand against his heart in that spontaneous manner. She felt safe and relaxed with Leif, a young man without foolish pretences and snobbery. She was sure he just liked her for herself. And that was something rare for a rich man's daughter.

15

For much of the evening Sir Alec contented himself with *The Old Curiosity Shop* and wrote a few obligatory postcards. Then, when that chore was out of the way, he decided to have a bath and retire early. Edward meanwhile devoured a Ruth Rendell mystery. As usual he read fast and overlooked several vital clues. The suspected mechanic turned out to be a red herring and Edward was annoyed with himself. He discarded the book, got up from his chair and glanced at his watch. It was late, and Juliet was not yet back. He was curious; *just going for a short walk*, she'd told her father. And Sir Alec had noticed that she'd taken the packet of shortbread with her, which was odd. She would hardly need them herself after the huge dinner they had consumed earlier. Was it a gift for someone and if so, who could she possibly know on the island? When she had bought them at the Wreck Museum he had assumed it was a gift for one of her friends in London, not someone on Scurra.

Edward adjusted his dark green tie, checked his watch against the time on the clock on the mantlepiece and got up. He was just about to go to his own room when he glanced across at Juliet's door. She was still out and Sir Alec was in the bath. He decided to take a risk on her not coming back at that moment. Deftly he crossed to her room and opened the door. The roses in the vase were wilting and there was a hint of lavender fragrance to the room.

Edward opened the top drawer of her dressing table. It contained some skimpy white underclothes. Edward closed the drawer and stood still for a few moments. Sir Alec had begun to let the bath water out. He reached down and opened the middle drawer. It contained Juliet's jumpers, a writing pad, sketch pad and her diary. He retrieved the diary, a small pocket book with a page for each day. Juliet had been meticulous in keeping up the entries, recording the events of each day in her small neat handwriting.

Edward turned to the last entry.

Fine sunny morning. Drove to local shop, meeting man I had met on ferry. Gave him lift back. Later walked along cliff path to Magswell Point. Spectacular views. Dad and E played golf am and went to the downs with E in the afternoon. Scurra is a lovely island but Dad is making things difficult. Why did he have to ask E?

Edward re-read the entry, closed the diary and replaced it in the drawer, taking care to put it back in the same position as he had found it. Moments later he was back in his own room.

He was not pleased. He thought back to the ferry. He'd been with her most of the time apart from when she spoke to a student about his wallet. Surely, she didn't mean him? He remembered her sketch of a man with a little beard. He vaguely recalled that this student, or whatever he was, had a ridiculous wispy beard. And he hated the current fashion for beards.

Edward crossed over to his window and pulled back the curtains. It was a still night and the moon a slender crescent. A van drove past the hotel with an old Rolling Stones song blaring from its open windows. And in the headlights of the van, heading towards the hotel, he caught sight of the unmistakable figure of Juliet with a man walking by her side. In the poor light, Edward could not make out who it was, except that in that momentary glance it seemed to be a scruffy individual in denims. Edward pushed back the curtains, sat on his bed and waited.

'Thank you for the tea,' said Juliet softly. 'I did enjoy it.'

'And thanks for the biscuits,' replied Leif. He paused and looked awkwardly at Juliet. He wanted to kiss her, but it was too soon. Maybe she sensed his desire and moved back a little. Leif glanced down, put his hand to his goatee beard, stroking it thoughtfully.

'I like that,' said Juliet.

'What?' asked Leif.

'Your beard. It's unusual. And it suits you.'

Leif grinned. 'It's a habit of mine. I tend to pull it when I'm thinking.'

'Thinking what?'

'Thinking I'd like to see you again.'

Juliet smiled. 'That would be nice.'

'Tomorrow?'

Juliet hesitated. 'I'm not quite sure of everyone's arrangements. It's Dad's holiday, really. We came to please him and keep him company. He hasn't been well, and he wanted to come here. He did say something about going out in the car.'

'Then what about the evening?'

'Maybe. Look, Leif, I'll see you when I can, that's a promise. I know where you are.'

'Then I'll be waiting.'

Juliet touched his hand with her own quickly, then turned and ran up the three steps of the Scurra Manor Hotel. Leif waited a few moments before starting back to the campsite. After he had gone just a little way he glanced back at the hotel. A light had just been switched on in one of the rooms on the second floor and he saw Juliet reach up and draw her curtains. He doubted whether she could have seen him and contentedly continued on his way.

Edward heard Juliet enter the suite and waited for her to go to her room. After a few moments he eased himself off his bed, left his room and crossed over to Juliet's door. He felt tempted to enter her room unannounced and question her about who she had just seen. Instead he knocked and waited for Juliet to answer. She had slipped off her jacket and stood barefoot wearing her neat cotton dress.

'I wanted to make sure you were all right. Your father and I were worried.'

'Amazing as it may seem to you and Dad, I am all grown up, Edward. As you can see, I'm fine, thanks.'

'You said you were just going out for a short time.'

'So, I was longer than I expected.'

'As long as you're all right.' He hesitated. 'Alec and I are playing golf in the morning. Then we thought we'd come back for you, have a pub lunch and see some more of the island.'

'I was intending to go—'

'Good,' cut in Edward. 'That's settled then.' He smiled at Juliet, bent over and kissed her lightly on the cheek. 'Good night,' he said and turned to go back to his own room.

Juliet slammed the door behind him. Edward chuckled. He liked a woman with character and Juliet certainly had character. That scruffy student didn't have a chance. She was just amusing herself.

16

Dizzy yawned, stretched and finally got up on all fours.

'Is it that time already?' asked Ann, glancing at her watch.

Dizzy barked in agreement. Ann put her embroidery down and prepared to go out. Without fail, the little spaniel always knew when it was 10 o'clock and rarely was he out by a few minutes.

She locked the cottage and with Dizzy walking by her side, the two set off down the village street to the junction where the antique shop was. They crossed the road and made their way down the alley to the playing fields, park and recreation area. It was there that Ann let Dizzy off his lead and with a yap of delight the spaniel bounded off into the dark.

It was a lonely and exposed spot, and many had warned her from going there at night but, apart from once disturbing a couple making love, most evenings passed without incident.

Ann usually stayed at the end of the alley observing the night sky and star formations. She recalled the ditty her mother had taught her: *'When the stars begin to huddle, the earth becomes a puddle.'*

And if the stars did seem closer together, Ann knew the next day would be wet. The stars rarely let her down.

On a moonlit night she could sometimes see the plateau containing the Seven Stones and, occasionally when it was full moon and the night was still, she could make out the gibbet silhouetted against the night sky, not that she looked too hard. Many a time she had spoken of her desire for the gibbet to be removed but hers had been a lone voice.

As the church clock chimed the half hour, Ann called to Dizzy. But the dog did not come. Ann called again.

There was no sound, no movement.

Ann whistled and called louder.

Still Dizzy did not appear.

Puzzled and a little anxious, Ann moved into the open field.

'Dizzy,' she called, her voice even louder.

She heard an owl and the screech of a car braking suddenly, but there was no sign of her little dog. There was no movement anywhere. Had there been a fox or some other animal after Dizzy she would have heard something. But it had all been so quiet.

'Dizzy!'

Ann continued further into the field. In the darkness she could make out the hedges that were at far end of the field. If need be she would walk right round. She was sure Dizzy would not leave the field. He never did. Wherever he went – and she was sure he had a favourite spot – he always returned moments after she had called.

Finally, she reached the hedge. She felt uneasy. Something had happened. Dizzy was not a dog to let her down.

Ann started to walk alongside the hedge, anxiously peering into the darkness. Several times she called out but there was no answer. All was still, all silent.

She said a prayer as she walked and then broke into a trot. She had to find her little dog.

'Dizzy,' she yelled. 'Dizzy, where are you?'

Then, faint and distant, she heard something. In the darkness, someone responded.

Ann started to run back across the field towards where she thought the voice was coming from. Several times she caught her breath. It had been years since she had last run and her heart thumped in her chest, protesting at the exertion. 'Dizzy? Dizzy!'

And out of the darkness she heard the familiar yap

and saw the little dog bounding towards her. Ann dropped to her knees and put her arms around the animal.

'Where ever have you been?' she panted. 'I've been so worried.'

Dizzy licked her, relishing the affection and cuddles he was receiving. 'Where ever have you been?' she repeated, resting her head lightly on the dog, content and relieved he was safe. As she caught her breath she became aware of someone approaching. The figure was walking slowly and in the dark she could just catch the gleam of a plastic carrier bag.

'Ma, is that you?' asked Ann warily.

'Aye,' replied the old woman, her voice coarse and penetrating.

Ma Demuth came nearer. In the darkness she looked more sinister than usual.

'I see you got your dog back.'

'Yes. Where was he?'

'Wanderin'' about in Lower Arch.' Ma sniffed. 'I guessed you was 'ere so I led 'im back.'

Ann gave Dizzy another tight squeeze. 'What were you doing in Lower Arch?' she whispered to the dog. 'You know you always wait for me.'

Dizzy whimpered, and Ann got to her feet.

'Well, thank you, Ma,' she said.

Ma stood still, watching Ann intently as she slipped on Dizzy's lead.

''as anything happened?' Ma asked.

'What?' enquired Ann.

'At the 'otel?'

'How do you mean?'

'Odd-like?'

Ann shook her head. 'No. Should there have been?'

'I 'eard Archie was called out.'

'Archie?'

Ma nodded. 'Archie Cann. He was told there was some knocking in one of the bedrooms.'

'Knocking?'

'In 'er room upstairs.' Ma paused. 'The dark 'aired girl what's staying at the 'otel.'

'I really don't know,' replied Ann. 'I don't know what you're talking about.'

Ma smiled. Her teeth, those that she had, were discoloured and seemed almost florescent in the moonlight. Her breath reeked of stale beer. The old woman moved forward and gripped Ann's arm. Ann tried to pull back, but the old woman's bony grip was vice-like.

'The knocking, it was in 'er room,' insisted Ma, ''er room upstairs.'

Ann pulled her arm free and edged away. 'Look, I don't know what you are going on about.'

'You will,' said Ma. 'Things are 'appening. Be warned. Things are 'appening. In 'er room upstairs.'

Ann Walker turned and headed back towards the alley. Had it been anyone else she would have thanked them more profusely for finding Dizzy but Ma Demuth was different. And she was suspicious. She was sure Dizzy wouldn't leave the field without her. Somehow the old woman had ensnared him. If only Dizzy could speak and tell her what had really happened.

And as she and Dizzy made their way back towards the alley they could hear the coarse laugh of Ma Demuth behind them, echoing through the still Scurra night.

17

Juliet did not go to sleep easily. Her mind was too active. The impudence of Edward – coolly leaning over and kissing her despite all the rude things she had said to him. He was just impervious to anything but his own vanity and power. She had to keep her distance.

She thought too of Leif. She was so glad she had met him. He kept things to himself but that added interest to his character. And Juliet was sure that behind his quiet, calm manner, there lurked a humorous, warm person. She smiled as she recalled his reluctance about telling her what *Leifu* was about. His poetry, his thoughts; there was depth to him and she liked a person who thought deeply, as she did herself. One day, maybe tomorrow, she would get him to read some.

Juliet heard the clock on St Michael's chime midnight and it was a little later when she finally gave way to sleep.

At 2:15 the tapping began. A gentle persistent tap, this time at the window.

Tap.

Tap.

TAP.

Juliet groaned, her eyes flickering a moment before drifting back to sleep.

Tap.

Tap.

TAP.

Sometimes soft, sometimes louder, but for fifteen long minutes it persisted. Then, at 2:30, it stopped, almost as suddenly as it had started.

All was quiet, all apart from Juliet's soft breathing and the faint whir of the clock radio.

At three o'clock the floral curtains in the bedroom began to quiver, just as if a gentle breeze were blowing through an open window or someone had brushed against them. But the windows were closed and there was no breeze. And the room began to get noticeably colder.

Juliet adjusted her sleeping position and buried her head deeper into her pillow.

The curtains moved again, this time more vigorously, the curtain hooks clicking as they lurched against the rail.

Juliet stirred and opened her eyes. She lay still for a moment, surprised at how cold she felt. She was sure it was the cold that had awakened her and she pulled the duvet up over her shoulders. It was then that she knew something was wrong, something was happening in her room.

She raised her head and immediately saw the movement in the curtains. She watched, frightened but mesmerised by the buffeting material. This was no dream. Something, someone was moving them.

Warily, Juliet eased herself out of her bed and crept over to the curtains. In one swift movement she yanked them apart. There was nothing – nothing but the closed windows, and the views of Hunter's Valley emerging out of the early morning mist. There was no draft, no obvious reason for the curtains to move. And her room had got so very cold.

Juliet checked her door. It was firmly shut. Had someone tried to enter, the draft of the door might have caused the curtains to move, but not as violently as she had seen. Juliet opened her door and then closed it. The curtains barely moved. Something, somebody had moved those curtains.

Juliet went over to her chest of drawers and took out a sweatshirt. She slipped it over her nightshirt, pulled the curtains firmly shut and then slipped back into bed, all the time watching the material. They were now still. And she vaguely recalled the tapping she had heard earlier in the night, a noise she had ignored in her sleepy state. She had heard tapping on the first night and had told Norman Strevans about it. But not like this. And the curtains had not moved then.

There was something very wrong with her room and she would speak to Strevans in the morning.

Edward knocked on Juliet's door. There was no answer. He glanced at his watch and then at Sir Alec.

'Juliet's usually up by now,' he declared.

Sir Alec frowned. 'I'll take a look,' he said and he quietly opened Juliet's door. Juliet was still in bed, sitting upright, with her head slouched forward. Her breathing was heavy.

'Is she all right?' enquired Edward.

Sir Alec moved over to Juliet's bedside and looked at his sleeping daughter. It was a curious position in which to sleep – as if she had been reading and had just dozed off. But there were no magazines or books around. Somehow Juliet had fallen asleep sitting upright.

'We'll leave her,' whispered Sir Alec. 'She's obviously tired. But it's not like her.'

The two men had breakfast and Sir Alec asked Elizabeth, one of the waitresses, for something to be put aside for Juliet, should she want breakfast.

When they returned to the suite they found it empty. Juliet had got up, dressed and gone.

'Strange,' said Edward, somewhat irritated.

Sir Alec reached for the phone and called reception.

Juliet saw Norman Strevans sitting in the office behind the reception desk. She slipped past the receptionist, busy pouring over a map with some guests, knocked at the door and entered.

'Mr Strevans,' she began.

Norman turned in his swivel chair and looked up at the young woman. She was pale and lacking the sparkle she had when he had first seen her.

'Miss Tyler,' he said. 'Is anything wrong?'

'Yes, there is,' replied Juliet. 'It's my room.'

He looked inquiringly at her. 'Go on.'

'Last night I had another disturbance. There was that tapping sound again and the curtains moved, as if someone was shaking them.'

Norman rolled his tongue around his mouth, a habit of his when searching for words. He found it a useful delaying tactic for awkward guests.

'Say that again,' he said. 'You heard taps and . . . and the curtains moved?'

'As if they were being shaken,' repeated Juliet. 'But there was no one there.'

The hotelier remained silent, fearing what she might say next.

'And I was not imagining it, either,' she continued. 'What's more, the room got very cold.'

'How very peculiar,' declared Norman thoughtfully.

'Look, I don't know it is or what's causing it, but has this ever happened before?'

Norman shook his head. 'No,' he said slowly. 'Not that I'm aware.' He paused, easing himself out of his chair. 'Now you say you saw the curtains move. Are you sure the windows were closed? Could they . . .' The hotelier stopped as Jill, one of the receptionists, entered the office.

'Excuse me,' Jill started, looking first at Norman Strevans and then at Juliet. She had been left in no doubt by Mrs Strevans of the importance of the hotel's present guests and she knew exactly who Juliet Tyler was. 'Excuse me,' she said again. 'I have Sir Alec on the phone. He was asking where you were, Miss.'

'Tell him I'll be coming in a moment.'

Jill nodded and left to relay the message.

'So,' resumed Norman, 'you're sure the windows were closed?'

'Mr Strevans, the windows were closed. The door was closed. But the curtains moved, and they moved violently. I could even hear the hooks shake against the rail.'

Norman rolled his tongue around his mouth once more, looking all the time at Juliet.

'I'll get a workman to have another look at your room. Just to check there are no drafts and the curtain rail is secure. I am sure there is some simple explanation. Now,' said Norman Strevans with a smile. 'Don't you worry about a thing, Miss Tyler. Enjoy your holiday and we'll sort out the problem.'

Juliet heard Edward's voice in the background. He had come down to the reception and was talking to Jill. It was typical of him to interfere. Juliet turned and left the small office, swept past Edward and back up the stairs. Edward followed her.

'What was all that about?' asked Jill, walking through to the office.

'It sounds as if she had a bad dream,' murmured the hotelier. 'If it was a dream.'

18

'Leif? Leif? Are you there?'

Leif finished pulling the cord on his small rucksack and backed out of his tent.

'I'm so glad,' declared Rose with some relief. 'For a moment I thought I missed you.'

Somewhat dishevelled, Leif struggled to his feet.

'No, I overslept. Guess it's all this fresh air.'

'That's what it is,' agreed Rose heartily. 'After a few days, it gets to you. Always does. I says there's no air better than Scurra air to relax you.' Rose smiled. 'Take them school children. They've quietened down no end. They always do after the first few days. Anyhow,' she continued. 'I've brought you a letter and piece of fruit cake. I always like to look after the young men on their own.' Rose chuckled. 'I knows how you tend to neglect yourself, skimping on food and the like.'

Leif grinned and took the cake, wrapped in a serviette, and the blue envelope that Rose handed him. From the Ipswich postmark and writing on the envelope it had to be from Aunt Agatha.

'That's most kind of you,' he said appreciatively. 'I like fruit cake.'

'It's always popular, my fruit cake,' said Rose proudly. 'So, where are you off to today?'

'Pear Beach.'

'Good grief, that's the last place I thought you'd go. It's all spoilt with them amusements and arcades. I always thought of you as a walker, not a beach-goer.'

'It's a nostalgic visit,' replied Leif. 'I once buried my dad in the sands there and I want to take another look.'

'You'll find it changed, that's for sure. They've spoilt it – used to be so nice. But it's like a lot of things, really. Things change and not always for the better,' Rose sighed, nodded her head thoughtfully and turned. 'Anyway, enjoy your walk,' she said and began to make her way back across the field.

Leif put the cake down and ripped open the envelope, surprised that his aunt had contacted him. He had not even given her the address of the campsite, so she must have found out from his mother. Inside was a twenty-pound note with a small piece of writing paper attached.

Dear Leif, the note began.

Mary told me where you were going and I hope the enclosed will come in useful.

Enjoy yourself but please DO be careful, Leif, please.

Love, Agatha.

Leif read the note several times and despite the generous gift – and it was generous – he was disturbed by what his aunt had written. Agatha, along with all her other eccentricities, considered herself a bit of a seer. She had vivid dreams and flashes of insight, or psychic impressions, as she called them. And he was certain she had received an impression concerning him. Why else would she have sent a letter? She had meant what she had written and it left him uneasy.

Aunt Agatha's hunches, dreams or psychic impressions, rarely let her down.

Edward Harrison pulled on one of the curtains in Juliet's room and watched the small ripples it created. He looked back at Juliet.

'Appears to be in order,' he declared.

'I knew you'd say that,' replied Juliet. 'All I can say is that something shook those curtains and there was a tapping at the window.'

'Sounds a bit unlikely,' queried Sir Alec. 'Are you

sure you weren't dreaming?'

'No, Dad, I definitely heard it.'

'And what did Strevans say?' enquired Edward.

'He said he would look into it, as he did before.' Juliet turned to her father standing in the doorway. He was looking at her thoughtfully.

'Well, let's hope he finds something,' he said and glanced at his watch. 'Anyway, time for golf, Edward. Then a pub lunch. All right, Juliet?'

Reluctantly she agreed. Sir Alec went through to his own room leaving Edward standing with his back against the curtains. He was watching her with that unnerving way he had as if trying to will her towards him.

'I suppose you think I'm making this up,' she said.

He moved forward and rested his hands on her shoulders. Juliet flinched but Edward's grip prevented her from moving back.

'Know what I think?' he asked. 'I think you're beautiful.'

'About this room,' Juliet said sternly.

Edward smiled. Like her father he found it hard to believe her description of the events of the night. 'If you're unhappy here,' he said quite seriously, 'you can always move in with me.'

'You must be joking,' said Juliet trying again to move away. Edward leant forward and kissed her firmly on the lips. She felt his arm around her waist pulling her towards him.

'No, Edward!'

He kissed her again. She struggled to get free but still he held her tightly.

'Why fight it?' he whispered. 'You can't win.' His lips found hers again and he kissed her, all the time pressing against her so that she could smell the aftershave he always wore and beneath this the slight smell of sweat and distinctive male odour. The feel of his solid, muscular body against her own, so obviously savouring her flesh and that growing hardness which he took no trouble to disguise made her shudder with fear and horror. She did NOT want this, not with this man.

Juliet jerked her head back, releasing herself from Edward's kiss.

'Edward,' she gasped. 'If you don't let go, I'll scream.'

'You wouldn't dare.'

Juliet took a deep breath and immediately Edward released her.

'Never, ever do that again!'

'This, my sweet, is just the beginning.'

'I'm telling you, Edward. If you dare touch me again, I'll tell my father.'

'Please do. He'll be delighted. He wants us to come together. And we will Juliet, we will.'

Forty minutes later Juliet dropped her father and Edward at the Scurra Golf Club. She was still angry with Edward and had spoken little since they had left the hotel.

'Meet you back here at one,' said her father and he gave her a kind and understanding smile. 'Take care, Juliet.'

She watched as Edward and her father made their way towards the club house. Her father limped slightly but she could see him smiling contentedly as he conversed with Edward. Maybe they were joking about the taps at the windows, the curtains or some business matter. What did it matter? She was furious with Edward – and annoyed with herself for letting it happen. The whole incident, Edward holding her tightly in his arms, kissing her, pressing against her body. . . it made her shudder again. She had to stop him before he did anything else. Surely her father wouldn't approve of this sort of behaviour? Surely, he cared about her feelings?

With a little sob of despair, she released the hand brake and drove out of the car park. She had no destination in mind and made her way towards the centre of the island, the part the guidebooks described as Secret Scurra. From the road she could see the plateau containing the Seven Stones and on the opposite side Gibbet Hill. She drove through Lower Arch and finally stopped at the Scurra General Stores.

She wondered if Leif had been into the shop again and if Steve, the old shopkeeper, was still mourning the loss of his dog. The old man was talking in a subdued voice to a customer and looked up as she entered. And the customer was that horrid, ragged old woman with a carrier bag by her feet, the same woman she had seen in the lane and who had frightened her so. The old woman stared at Juliet with her dark eyes before turning back to the shopkeeper.

19

The sign stood prominently on the seafront.

WELCOME TO PEAR BEACH

The lettering was in a garish yellow against a blue background and painted in the top right corner was a bronzed holidaymaker relaxing in a deck chair. A welter of beach cafes, ice-cream kiosks and amusement arcades lined the seafront with a motley collection of shops, their entrances cluttered with beach balls, sand toys and racks of postcards. An amusement arcade, with flashing lights and advertising the latest in video games, stood at the end of the seafront and outside were a cluster of teenagers eating candyfloss.

Families, many struggling with young children and bags stuffed with beachwear and toys, made their way along the seafront to the steps that led down to the beach.

Leif walked slowly, regarding the scene with interest. He noticed a small tower; inside was a graph showing the temperatures recorded so far in the month and another showing the temperatures the same month a year ago. The tower seemed to have been there for many years but Leif didn't remember it. Nor did he remember the gaudy cafés or the many hotels and guesthouses he passed on his way to the beach. All he remembered was burying his father in the sand and the walk to the ice-cream shop.

He jumped the short distance from the esplanade to the sand. A deck chair attendant was adding another row to the yellow and blue deck chairs. It was going to be a hot and busy day.

Leif weaved his way between the rows of chairs. A toddler collided with him and was quickly retrieved by a despairing mother. Leif noticed two deeply tanned teenage girls lying on the beach, listening to their music, and oblivious to all around them.

He continued beyond the chairs. The tide was still going out, revealing yet more of the stretches of beach that made Pear Beach so famous. The sand under Leif's feet was already dry and soft and he knelt down and scooped up some of the golden grains and watched as they trickled between his fingers. And as the sand fell he tried to imagine himself on his last visit.

He'd been six then. Fair, skinny and with a mischievous grin, which he remembered his granny calling 'right royal impish.' And he would have revelled in his island holiday. Almost every day he would have begged his parents to take him to the beach and most days they would have taken him. He would have had his bucket and spade and would have decorated his castles with colourful paper flags. And he had this one memory of burying his father. He had started with his feet and moved up his legs, piling on more and more sand. His father had pretended to be asleep and Leif remembered squealing in delight at the mischief he was up to. No doubt his mother had helped him in his escapade.

Then he remembered his father opening his eyes and his look of feigned amazement when he found himself buried under so much sand. He lay there open-mouthed and Leif had laughed with joy while his mother had taken a picture. Several pictures; one of Leif proudly kneeling by his father, both grinning at the camera, and another shot of Leif with his arm around his father. It was a happy moment. And one of their last. No one knew of the cancer that was already tearing into Peter Olsen and that was to destroy him in a matter of weeks.

From that happy moment it seemed such a short step to the time when his father was rushed to hospital and the doctor telling him that his daddy was very poorly. That they might not be able to make him better.

Leif's eyes filled with tears as the vivid and painful memory returned to him. He had loved his father – or the memory that he had of him. He felt that he had to live up to his father's expectations and it hadn't always been easy. His years at school were mediocre and it was only in the sixth form that he had begun to make a marked improvement. Through sheer hard work and determination, he had managed to get the necessary grades and, against all expectations, secured a place at the University of Bournemouth. Obtaining a BA would make his Mum feel so proud and he'd feel Dad would be proud too, wherever his spirit may be now.

So much depended on the result. At twenty-two, his future, his whole life, lay before him.

Leif scooped up more of the sand and stared at the tiny particles he held. There was a small white shell amongst them and he pulled it from the sand and put it in his pocket. It would be a souvenir of Pear Beach.

A little distance away some children were peering into a pool of water, looking for any treasures the sea had left behind. Leif had vague recollections of another occasion, when he had found a starfish in a pool and shouting at the top of his voice about his discovery. His mother had come running and in the end there were about eight people gazing at the strange hapless creature.

Leif sighed. Perhaps it had been wrong to come back and wallow in the memories. Pear Beach had changed and been spoilt. Maybe it was best to leave the past where it belonged, to remember the happy times and look to the future. But then this visit had been a sort of pilgrimage. A journey to where he could remember the distant and happy memories of his father. It was a journey that had to be made in order to let go.

Leif closed his eyes. 'God bless you, Dad,' he murmured, and he stayed kneeling at that spot for a few minutes, oblivious to the laughter of excited children, the music from a transistor and chatter from the holidaying crowd around him. He prayed and thought of his father. Only the light touch of a hand upon his shoulder disturbed him.

Leif opened his eyes and found Juliet kneeling beside him. She smiled but said nothing. Leif looked at her, aware his eyes were still moist.

'Is this where you played sand games with your father?' she asked quietly.

Leif nodded. 'How did you know?'

'Rose told me. I went to the campsite to see if you were there.'

Leif looked back at the sand and idly scooped up more, letting it trickle through his fingers, thinking how life trickled away like this.

'It's a bit of a nostalgic visit,' he started. 'It's . . . it was one of the last memories of my father. He died soon after we came here.'

Leif felt Juliet's hand press reassuringly on his shoulder. Leif turned to her and gazed into her hazel eyes.

'Past days of sunshine
of happiness and of joy
casting their warmth ... forever.'

Juliet regarded Leif thoughtfully. 'Whose words are they?'

'I'll tell you one day,' he replied. 'Come. Let's go.'

Juliet got to her feet and Leif eased himself up only to buckle over again.

'Ouch,' he cried, grimacing and smiling at the same time. 'Pins and needles,' he explained and wobbled his way uneasily over the soft sand while Juliet giggled. He reached for her hand and together they headed back to the esplanade.

'I know a nice tea garden,' he said. 'Would you like to go?'

Juliet nodded and they made their way to the Rolls. Leif did not look back at Pear Beach. He had made his pilgrimage. And felt curiously at peace.

'I came here the other day,' said Leif, leading Juliet round to the back of Heaven's Drop Tea Garden. Juliet went over to the flower border, admiring the red hot pokers and smelling the wild rambling roses.

'It's idyllic,' she murmured.

Leif agreed, and he watched as Juliet reached over for a white rose and smelt it. He wanted to take Juliet, to hold her in his arms and gaze into her eyes. She was special and so different from any one else he had met but she was surely older and so much more worldly wise than he was. He lowered his eyes and felt sad.

Juliet turned and looked at Leif. 'Why are you sighing like that?' she asked softly.

Leif shrugged his shoulders, their eyes meeting. Somehow there was no need for words. It was as if she understood his thoughts for she said quietly, 'I'll be twenty-four soon. It's my birthday in a week's time.'

'I'm twenty-three in a month's time,' said Leif.

'I thought you were a bit older than that.'

'It's the beard,' he said and they both smiled.

'But you're still studying?'

'I've finished and await the results. I couldn't bear to hang about in suspense, so I decided to pack my rucksack and come here. Get away from it all.'

'Sensible.'

Leif looked away and gazed into the distance.

'And I've always considered Scurra special. But ...' Leif trailed off and, for a moment, the two sat in silence, locked in thought.

The proprietor approached their table. Today he wore an apron with FRANKIE emblazoned on it. 'So,' he asked. 'What would you like?'

'Coffee, please,' Juliet replied.

'Filtered, instant, decaffeinated, Cappuccino, white, black, cream or milk?'

Juliet laughed. 'Spoilt for choice,' she murmured, catching sight of Leif's grin.

They both gave their order and waited for Frankie to go.

'It's always an inquisition,' explained Leif. 'Last time I had to decide between varieties of teas, some I'd never heard of.'

'But it's nice here. Thanks for bringing me.'

'And thank you for finding me,' he said, and he reached across and took Juliet's hand. 'Tell me, is anything wrong?'

'How do you mean?'

'Well, you must have gone to some effort to find me.'

Juliet shook her head. 'No, there's nothing wrong.'

'That tells me there is,' replied Leif. 'An aunt of mine taught me some things about body language. And when someone shakes their head like that, it means they're hiding something.'

'Your aunt's perceptive.'

'Among other things. But I'm right, something is troubling you, isn't it?'

Juliet sighed. 'It's nothing, really.'

'I think it is. Please tell me.'

Juliet looked at him, studying his earnest features. 'It's . . . it's . . .' she hesitated. 'Leif, I'm scared you wouldn't understand.'

'Try me,' he said. 'Look Juliet, I might be able to help. I'd like to.'

Frankie approached the table carrying two steaming mugs of Cappuccino and a plate of homemade shortbread biscuits, cut into thick chunks. He seemed a little more cheerful today.

'Lovely day, my dears,' he said putting the tray on the table. 'Hope you enjoy it.'

They waited until he had gone.

'Please tell me,'

Juliet took a deep breath. 'It's just that there's something odd about my room.'

'At the hotel?'

She nodded. 'It started with some tapping early one morning. I thought it was the pipes. But last night I woke up with a start. The room was cold, really cold, just as if it was winter and the window had been left open. And I think the tapping started again. But what really frightened me were the curtains. The curtains started to move, slowly at first but then they started to shake, as if someone was tugging them. Yet when I went to look there was no one there.'

'And the windows were shut?'

'Definitely. There was no reason for them to move.' Juliet hesitated. 'You do believe me, don't you?'

Leif squeezed Juliet's hand reassuringly.

'I do,' he said. 'Have you told anyone?'

'I told the hotel manager about the tapping I heard on the first night. He got a plumber to check for air-locks, but he didn't find anything. And this morning I told him about the curtains.'

'What did he say?'

'He said he would look into it.' Juliet paused. 'And I told Dad and Edward.'

'Edward?'

Juliet nodded. 'My father's adviser. Horrid man.'

Leif hesitated, as he recalled his first meeting with Juliet. How she had told him about his wallet and how he had seen her go off to a man waiting for her. He had forgotten all about him.

'Was he the man on the ferry?' Leif asked.

Juliet nodded. 'My dad has thoughts of me marrying him. Some hope. I hate him.'

Leif took a shortbread and snapped it in two.

'So, what did your father and this Edward say?'

'They didn't believe me. They wouldn't. They won't believe anything that can't be explained. They just think it was a bad dream. But it wasn't, Leif, it wasn't!'

He reached for her hand once more.

'I believe you,' he said. 'And I'm beginning to think there's more to this island than meets the eye. I mean, I thought I saw a body hanging from the gibbet and there's that wretched tramp of a woman, Ma Demuth.'

'The one with the carrier bag?'

Leif nodded. 'The barman at the Compass says she's psychic. And the other night when I was there, she just kept staring at me.'

'Maybe she stares at everyone. She gave me that awful fright in the lane last night and she stared at me this morning. I went into the shop and she was talking to the shopkeeper. As soon as she saw me she whispered, "That's 'er, Mr Games. That's who I was telling you about." And when she left the shop you should have seen the look the shopkeeper gave me. He looked terrified of me. As if I had some sort of contagious disease.'

'I think she gives everyone the creeps.' Leif sipped his coffee. 'And to add to all this, I received this note this morning.' Leif took out his wallet and removed the money Aunt Agatha had sent, still with the piece of paper attached. Leif passed it to Juliet. 'It's from one of my aunts.'

Juliet read the message. 'What does she mean, "do be careful"?'

Leif shrugged his shoulders. 'I don't know. But

Aunt Agatha is . . . well, she thinks she's psychic. She wouldn't have written without good cause. But it's odd, just the same.'

Juliet ran her hand through her long black hair, all the time looking at Leif. 'So, what do you make of all this?' she finally asked.

'I wish I knew,' he sighed. 'Anyway, let's not think about it anymore. I mean, it's a lovely day and we're here amongst all this beauty.'

She smiled uncertainly but despite the warmth of the sun and serenity of the surroundings, she shivered.

'Leif,' she whispered. 'You will do as your auntie asks, won't you?'

'What?'

'Be careful.'

'Yes, yes, I will . . . but of what?'

'Promise?'

Leif looked inquiringly at Juliet. 'Why, do you believe in what she says?'

'I'm afraid I do, Leif. And I'd hate anything to happen.'

20

Sir Alec positioned the ball on the tee and took out his five iron. He liked the eighth hole. Challenging but satisfying.

He took a deep breath, gripped the club and took a practice swing. Edging closer to the ball, he raised his club and struck. The ball shot in the air and arched high above the course before descending. From where Sir Alec and Edward stood it was a mere speck, but it seemed to have landed just right of the bunker, ideally placed for the green.

'Good shot,' said Edward approvingly. They both reached for their trolleys and began to make their way to the distant balls.

Although just mid-morning it was already sticky. There was little breeze and the course lay in the full sun.

Sir Alec glanced at his watch. His leg was bothering him and the heat made him uncomfortable. He felt thirsty, tired and old. Ever since the coronary last year, he had felt himself slowing down. Everything was much more effort and he realised more than ever that he had to enjoy life while he still could.

Halfway to the green, Sir Alec stopped and gazed over the course to the sea beyond. A ferry was heading towards Narraport and a half-empty launch ploughed through the sea, taking people to one of the other islands.

Edward joined Sir Alec and the two men stood in silence for a few moments, both admiring the shimmering sea; the sea that John Steelgate had so vividly captured in the painting that hung at the hotel.

'Alec,' asked Edward suddenly, 'why did you choose Scurra?'

Sir Alec drew a deep breath, feeling the fresh Scurra air fill his aged lungs. 'Because I like the place,' he replied. 'Always have.'

'You've been here before?'

Sir Alec nodded. 'Many years ago, with my dear wife. I liked it then and I vowed one day I would come back.'

Edward decided not to enquire further, and Sir Alec said no more.

A speedboat pulling a water-skier rounded the headland. The skier zigzagged over the waters, enjoying the challenge. Edward watched approvingly. The skier was good and Edward respected those who had perfected their craft.

'Edward,' said Sir Alec at last. 'About Juliet.'

'Yes?' Edward enquired, still focused on the skier.

'What do you feel about her?'

Edward hesitated a moment. 'How exactly do you mean?'

'Do you care for her?'

'Of course.' Edward turned to Sir Alec. 'You know I do.'

'And does she care for you?'

'Oh, I'm sure she does. She likes playing hard to get but I'm sure she does care.'

'I hope so,' smiled Sir Alec. 'My wife kept me guessing for a long while. I had plenty of rivals. She was a real beauty.' He sighed a little. 'Juliet takes after her in looks, thank goodness. And I like to think she has some of my business savvy too. But she's young and ... well, I'm not sure I fully understand her. Or what she wants from life.'

'Do we ever understand women? Or they, us?''

Sir Alec laughed. 'Fair point.' He hesitated and added, 'What do you make of this business last night?'

'You mean the noises and the curtains?'

Sir Alec nodded.

'I don't know. May have been a dream or maybe she's just tired. Got too uptight about those illustrations she completed for the exhibition last month.'

'Edward, if anything happens to me, I want you to look after her. To take care of her, you understand?'

'But nothing is going to—'

'Edward,' interrupted Sir Alec. 'I'm telling you this while I can. God alone knows how long I've got. But when I go, I want you to look after her, you understand?'

The young man nodded.

'I've made a new will and . . .' Sir Alec paused. 'You know Andrew, my solicitor?'

'Yes.'

'I've been through everything with him. He'll take care of most things. Juliet shouldn't have too much worry.'

'And your interests?'

'I want you to manage them on her behalf. Ultimately it will be her decision as to what happens. But,' Sir Alec looked earnestly at Edward, 'I want you to get to know her better. She seems tough, but she's very sensitive. She needs a husband, Edward. She needs someone she can rely on.'

Edward smiled. 'She would make a beautiful wife,' he said.

And a rich one, he thought to himself as the two men continued their game.

Unlike some who had occupied the Dickens Suite, the present occupants left things immaculate. All their rooms were tidy and the many books they had brought with them were all neatly stacked in separate piles. Edward Harrison's room, however, resembled more an office than a bedroom. His state of the art computer took precedence on the dressing table with his expensive toiletries pushed to one side.

Ann Walker chose not to dust too much of Edward's room in case she disturbed anything. She did not care much for modern technology and feared the slightest touch might render the machines useless.

'It's a mighty fine holiday he's having,' Ann observed. 'You'd have thought he'd want to leave all this behind.'

Cherie, who came from Lyon and whose English was not good, nodded. ''E's a . . . what you say? A workolic?'

Ann laughed. 'Yes, definitely a workaholic!'

Together they moved on to clean Sir Alec's room. It was a cheery room with pale blue patterned wallpaper, dark blue curtains and dominated by the rocking chair Katherine Strevans had insisted on placing in the room.

A copy of *The Old Curiosity Shop* lay on the bedside table with a leather bookmark sticking up from the middle of the book. Sir Alec's neatly folded silk pyjamas lay under his pillow and his slippers were tucked just under the bed.

Ann approved of Sir Alec. She had read much about him in newspapers and magazines and he had always come across as a kindly benevolent figure. But she wondered whether, behind all his geniality, he was a lonely man. He had never remarried after his first wife had died and apart from his daughter he appeared to have no one.

After Sir Alec's room, Ann moved on to clean the smallest of the three bedrooms. Juliet's room, decorated in pastel pink, Ann remembered how she had helped Katherine choose the new curtains. Surprisingly, it was her choice that prevailed – it was unusual for Katherine to allow herself to be over-ruled – and the pretty floral material she chose did fit in well with the room.

Ann took the remaining roses from the vase and picked up some petals that had fallen on the dressing table and floor. Strangely, they had not lasted long and she decided to replace them with some sweet peas from the garden.

Like her father, Juliet kept her room tidy. Everything

had been put away and her silk nightshirt was tucked neatly under the pillow. Ann plucked a strand of Juliet's long hair from the pillow and as she did so the words of Ma Demuth suddenly returned to her.

That dark 'aired girl what's staying at the 'otel . . . Ann tried to put the wretched nosey old woman out of her mind. She was always going around trying to be mysterious and witchy and people actually believed some of her wilder stories. She caused nothing but trouble.

'Damn woman!' declared Ann to herself.

Cherie now walked in the room armed with a new liner for the bin.

'Almost done,' Ann announced.

Cherie frowned and looked around.

'What's the matter?' Ann asked, wondering what was puzzling her helper.

'Is nothing.'

'You're sure?'

Cherie hesitated. 'I am silly. I think someone was 'ere with you. Standing behind you, watching. Someone with dark hair, *oui,* just like Mademoiselle Tyler. For a minute I think she is in her room with you. But . . .' Cherie shrugged her shoulders and smiled. 'But there is no one.'

'No, there isn't. You probably heard me grumbling to myself,' said Ann sharply. And as she turned to leave the room, she shivered. And suddenly felt very uneasy.

21

It was just after one o'clock when Juliet pulled up outside the club house. Sir Alec and Edward came out of the foyer with Edward looking pointedly at his watch.

'Thought you were never coming,' he said.

Juliet ignored the remark and waited for them both to get in the car. She drove straight to the Windmill Inn, a sixteenth-century thatched building she had passed earlier, and all three sampled an ample Scurra Ploughman's.

'Right,' declared Sir Alec, finishing his coffee. 'According to the guide, today is market day.'

'*Market* day?' queried Edward.

'Not your everyday market,' continued Sir Alec, ignoring Edward's disdain. 'This is Scurra's summer market. The stallholders will be in costume and there'll be crafts, local produce and, according to the guide, plenty of antiques.'

Juliet nodded approvingly. 'I'd like to go,' she said. 'Where is it?'

'In the old quarters of Narraport, where the fish market used to be.' Sir Alec paused. 'I don't know if you remember the film *Call of the Sea Witch*, but part of it was filmed in the market.'

'The bit where Winston Cooper met that fisherwoman?' enquired Juliet.

Sir Alec nodded.

'Then I'd like to see it,' said Juliet enthusiastically. 'I really enjoyed that film.'

'That's settled then,' said Sir Alec rising from his seat. 'Let's be off.'

Juliet got up and followed her father towards the door. Edward reluctantly followed behind.

Parking was difficult in Narraport on market day and Edward, who drove, eventually had to settle on the outskirts of the town. They walked slowly through the streets, passing many well-known stores and occasionally stopping to look at displays in the shop windows.

The high street was pedestrianised and Sir Alec walked ahead with Juliet and Edward behind. Edward kept close to Juliet, often glancing at her. Since this morning, when she had appeared so tense, she now appeared a good deal more relaxed. The colour had returned to her face and she was more at ease.

Edward gestured towards a high-quality dress shop. He did not care for the garments on display but could see, from the prices, they were of the highest quality.

'These are nice,' he remarked casually.

Juliet glanced over at the window but without great interest.

'Blue's your colour. The blue outfit there would suit you,' he added. 'Would you like me to buy it for you?'

'I don't think so,' said Juliet.

'Oh, come on, Juliet, don't be so cruel. Show me some feeling!' He tried to put his arm around her waist. Juliet wriggled free and gave him a withering look.

'I warned you! Edward, get it in your head, there is no feeling in me for you but one of dislike!'

'But I love you,' he whispered. The words fell uneasily from his lips.

Juliet ignored him and ran a few paces to join her father. She held his arm until they were at the market.

Although the market had been open since early morning, it was still busy. The stalls were laid out in four rows in a large cobbled square. Most of them had blue and white canopies draped over the frames to protect the stallholders from the sun. A blind accordion player stood at the end of one of the rows playing sea shanties. A guide dog lay dutifully at his master's feet and in front of the dog was a peaked cap containing a generous collection of English and foreign coins. Juliet dropped a few coins in the cap, and the sleepy dog looked up and blinked. Edward and Sir Alec added to the collection. The blind man, hearing the chink of metal, smiled contentedly and played on.

The stalls sold a wide range of items. Several specialised in local confectionery and boxes of Scurra fudge, in all its many flavours, was in great demand. So too was Scurra Dairy Ice Cream, and several children frantically licked at their dripping cones to prevent the melting ice cream from being lost on the cobbles.

The fruit and vegetable stalls were also busy, many attracted by the lively patter of a heavily tattooed stallholder, while the stalls selling small pottery figures, local lace and dried flower arrangements were doing brisk trade with the souvenir hunters. Most of the stallholders were in Scurra costume, the ladies wearing frilly blouses and black skirts edged with lace trim while the men wore blue and white striped shirts and baggy black trousers.

Sir Alec made for a bookstall selling second hand books, remainders and a few bestsellers. He glanced over the stall and extracted a slim volume from the children's section and held it up for Juliet to see. It was *The Yestermorrow Man* and a sticker had been placed on the cover mentioning the two awards the book had already won. Under the author's name was *Illustrated by Juliet Tyler*.

'Aren't you proud?' Sir Alec whispered. 'Your mother would be.'

'I didn't expect to see a copy here,' smiled Juliet.

Edward wandered off to an antique stall. Most was overpriced although the quality was generally good. Edward picked up two of the horse brasses on display and examined them. Juliet flicked through a box of prints. They were mainly of animals, birds and flowers.

'Anything in particular?' asked the stallholder, a man with a bushy ginger beard and wearing Scurra costume.

Juliet shook her head.

'There's more prints in here,' he said eagerly and produced a smaller box from under the table. 'Prints of Scurra. Make lovely presents, love.' The man turned to Edward. 'Lovely pieces, them brasses. Good value, too.' he said.

Juliet looked at the box. There were prints of St Nicholas church at Narraport, the fish market when it was a fish market, boats moored in the old harbour, Scurra rock and many prints of the Seven Stones and with the gibbet in the distance. Juliet noticed that one of the prints of the stones was by John Steelgate, the only print by him in the box.

'Lovely one that is,' added the stall keeper. 'And by a fine artist. The best Scurra had.'

Juliet nodded non-committedly.

'If you're interested in Steelgate I've got a book of his work. Limited edition and very rare.'

The proprietor once more burrowed under the table, this time retrieving a large book covered in bubble wrap. Through the plastic bubbles Juliet could read the title, *The Collected Paintings of John Steelgate*.

'Are you interested?' asked the stallholder, holding the book with care. 'It's a lovely book. Good value and a real collector's item.' He eased the bubble wrap from off the book and flicked through the pages for Juliet to see. Many were in colour and were a mixture of watercolours and oil paintings. As he turned the pages, Juliet caught glimpse of the painting of the Scurra rock, the same one that hung in the hotel. At a glance it looked an admirable collection.

'How much is it?' asked Juliet.

The stall keeper pursed his lips and looked at Juliet thoughtfully.

'For you, love, I'll make a special deal,' he said but

the price was still far greater than Juliet had expected and she shook her head.

'I'll tell you what,' he continued. 'If you're really interested, I'll knock a tenner off. How about that?'

'Done,' said Edward. 'And I'll take these three brasses as well.'

Edward reached for his wallet and took out several notes.

'A present,' he said, smiling at Juliet. 'A souvenir of our holiday.'

Juliet sighed and watched the stall keeper re-wrap the book, put some tissue paper round the brasses and sort out the change. When the transaction was complete, Edward handed the book to Juliet.

'For you, my dear,' he said and before Juliet could move he kissed her on her cheek.

'Thank you,' she mumbled rather ungraciously. 'I wonder where my father is?' She held the book tightly in her hands, pleased with it but wishing she had bought it herself.

'He's over there,' replied Edward, and he pointed to Sir Alec looking at a stall selling cards and stationary. He was clutching a brown paper bag in his hand.

'Bought something, Dad?' enquired Juliet, joining her father.

Sir Alec turned and smiled. He had a mischievous twinkle in his eye, like a child with a new toy.

'Yes,' he said. 'Some pencil rubbers.' And he reached in the bag and took them out. They had been cut and painted to resemble old books. On the front of one was printed *Great Expectations* and on the other *Pickwick Papers*.

'I think they are rather splendid,' he declared, chuckling contentedly.

Juliet, wearing her favourite batik skirt and lacy cream

blouse, lay on her bed. It was half an hour before supper. Edward was already changed and studying stock prices while Sir Alec lay in the bath reading.

Juliet undid the bubble wrap around her new book. Under the title was a picture of a gaunt bearded man who stared impassively from the cover.

The collection opened with an appreciation of Steelgate's career by Sir Andrew Amos followed by a detailed account of Steelgate's life. Juliet decided to leave the text to another occasion and turned to the main section of the book; the paintings.

The collection was roughly in date order and his early work was distinctly amateurish. It was only as he reached middle age that his true genius began to emerge.

Juliet paused a moment at the painting of the Hunter family, the same one that hung in the hotel lounge. All four Hunters stared back at her from the page, the young Hunter girl being the only one with a hint of a smile upon her face. On the adjoining pages were paintings of other Island families, all commissions that the young artist had eagerly accepted. Another was of Andrew Squires, a tall, proud and distinguished figure who, the caption said, was a frequent visitor to Scurra and later became Lord Tetherington, the Victorian Industrialist. There was also a painting of Dickens on Scurra – she would show that to her father – and then there were the many seascapes, most with a shimmering glow that seemed so much a hallmark of the artist.

Towards the back of the collection Juliet found some watercolours of the Seven Stones. One showed the stones at sunset with the red sun disappearing behind the seventh stone. Another was of the stones in springtime with a cluster of daffodils around them. In the background were the rolling downs with flocks of sheep grazing on the downland grass. At the top of the down, and clearly seen against the spiralling white clouds, was the Scurra gibbet. Hanging from

the gibbet was a body.
    Amid all the beauty and serenity of Scurra lurked the unmistakable shadow of death.

22

Leif squatted outside his tent and unfolded the lettercard he had bought for Aunt Agatha. He started by thanking her for the money and went on to describe some of the places he had visited. Soon three-quarters of the card had been written and Leif paused, wondering how to broach the warning she had given in her note. The warning had been troubling him and now it concerned Juliet too. Something had obviously prompted his aunt to contact him.

Leif put the pen and card down a moment and scrabbled back into the tent to slip on the sweatshirt he had been using as a pillow. He then rummaged in one of his bags and took out a bar of fruit and nut chocolate. It had melted during the day but had hardened again into a curious arc formation. Leif was just about to unwrap the bar when he heard a rustling outside his tent.

Intrigued, he pushed the flap door to one side and crawled out. Juliet stood to one side, watching him with a beaming smile on her face.

'I didn't expect to see you tonight,' he declared, scrabbling to his feet.

'I've come for some of your special brew,' said Juliet. 'Besides, I fancied a walk after supper.'

Leif brushed himself down. 'Had I known, I'd have changed into my tuxedo.'

Juliet laughed.

'It's lovely to see you, though.' He hesitated. 'I can't offer you a seat,' he said. 'More like – take a jumper.'

He retrieved another sweatshirt from his tent and spread it out. 'Here, you can sit on this.'

'I'm fine,' said Juliet, kneeling down. 'The grass is dry.'

Leif knelt opposite her, their knees almost touching.

They looked at each other. For a moment, neither spoke.

'I'm glad you've come,' he whispered. 'I take it you didn't see that old woman in the lane again?'

Juliet shook her head, glancing at the almost completed lettercard. 'You've written a lot. An admirer?' she asked with a smile.

'Of sorts. It's to my Aunt Agatha. I was writing to thank her for the money. And to ask her what she meant about my being careful.' Leif paused. 'I suppose there's always a chance we are reading too much into her words.'

'And maybe there's some simple explanation about what happened in my room.'

Leif took Juliet's hand and gently squeezed it a moment before scrabbling to his feet. 'I'll get the tea on,' he said and retrieved the camping stove and water bottle from just inside the fly sheet. He poured some water into his pan and lit the stove.

'What did you do this afternoon?'

'I went to Scurra market. It was fun on the whole. And you?'

'I did the cliff walk. From Heaven's Drop to Blue Point and then back here. It was a good walk.'

'And you've caught the sun,' Juliet observed, watching as Leif adjusted the flame. 'Leif, when you leave here, what are you going to do?'

He turned and looked at her. 'A lot depends on my degree. If I pass I've been offered a job at Sibley's.'

'The publishing company?'

Leif nodded. 'Ultimately I want to have my own publishing firm. But first I need to learn the trade.'

'What division will you be in?'

'It's a new section they're setting up. They're aiming to republish some Victorian books and it will be my job to source titles, amongst other things.'

'You know something about Victorian literature,

then?'

'I studied some for my degree. But, as I say, the job hinges on my results.'

Juliet smiled. 'And would they be interested in *Leifu*?'

'I doubt it.'

'Will you read me some?'

'Some time,' replied Leif teasingly. He reached over for the flask cups, tea bags and powdered milk.

'Go on,' she pleaded. 'Please.'

'You'll think it silly.' He poured the hot water into the flask cups.

'I won't.' She edged towards him and put her hand on his knee. 'I'd like to know, Leif. Honestly, I would.'

Leif turned and looked at her. Her hazel eyes gazing inquiringly into his. Her hand, although just resting on his knee, felt so delicate. For a moment they both were quiet and still, just looking at each other. And then Leif leant forward and kissed her. Her lips were soft, tender and receptive, her breath sweet and warm. He drew away and they gazed at each other.

Juliet cast her eyes down for a moment and couldn't help but think how natural and gentle this kiss was and how she welcomed and enjoyed it. Not like the rough and disgusting attentions of that wretched Edward.

'You aren't angry?' asked Leif, looking worried. 'Am I being forward?'

'No! Of course you're not. I liked it very much.'

'I sort of feel . . . I mean you're so much more . . . more worldly than me. I mean you must move in different circles and know such a lot of men . . .'

'Shush.' She placed a finger on his lips. 'You're reading me all wrong. I may be wealthy but I'm not worldly, not at all. Nor is my Dad, not really. He's always giving his money away, bless him. I don't care if he gives it all away. I like a simple life – I like being with you, Leif.'

'Truly?'

'Yes, truly.'

He coloured slightly with pleasure and her heart warmed to him even more. There was something so boyish about him.

Leif extracted the tea bags from the flask cups and added some powdered milk and handed her a mug. She took it and smiled.

'Okay, now tell me about *Leifu*?'

'My, you're persistent.'

Juliet nodded. 'I am. So, what is it?'

'It's based on *haiku*,' he finally said. 'True *haiku* contain references to nature, but mine is an inspirational variety.'

'Like the words you said on Pear Beach?'

'You remembered?'

'Of course, it sounded apt and beautiful.'

Leif looked at her with increasing admiration. He took the blue notebook from under the lettercard and opened it. Throughout the pages were some seventy verses, all carefully copied from the scraps of paper he had compiled them on. He selected one.

'*Took the nowhere road.*
Glad I did. I saw no one.
But I met myself.'

Juliet nodded appreciatively.

'Intriguing,' she declared with a smile. 'And another?'

Leif turned the pages, scanning the verses he had written.

'*I slept well last night.*
And dreamt impossible dreams
I made possible.'

'I like that,' said Juliet.

Leif closed his notebook. 'So now you know.'

They both finished their tea and from a kneeling position Juliet stretched her legs out before her and turned and gazed at the hill behind them and at the gibbet. Leif noticed some loose grass stuck to her legs and reached over and plucked some of the blades from her skin. Juliet turned back to Leif.

'Do you like sleeping so close to that thing?' she enquired.

'The gibbet? I don't much *like* it, but at least I'm in this field on my own.'

'I've got a book of some local paintings. There was one of the Seven Stones with the downs and gibbet in the background. And you can just make out a body hanging from the gibbet.'

'I think there often were. They hung them as deterrents.'

Juliet shivered.

They drank their tea and though they now both fell silent, lost in their own thoughts, there was a sense of companionship in it, a comfortable feeling of peace.

'It's getting late,' murmured Leif. 'I'll walk you back to the hotel.'

He quickly tidied up his things, secured the padlock and they began the walk back to the hotel. Leif clasped her hand and they ambled along the road feeling contented and happy.

'Have you any plans for tomorrow?' asked Leif.

'Not as yet.'

'Then how about us going for a walk? Maybe the coastal path?'

'I'd like that,' said Juliet. They came in view of the hotel lights. 'I'll come to the campsite tomorrow morning, about ten.'

'I'm looking forward to it already,' said Leif quietly.

'It's been a lovely evening. Thank you for coming tonight.'

'I've enjoyed it too,' she whispered. She reached up and removed a strand of grass from Leif's jumper. 'And I love *Leifu*,' she added. 'Write one for me.'

Leif reached over and taking her into his arms, held her against him gently and kissed her again. His kiss was light and gentle, soft against her own lips. They stood kissing like this for several moments and Juliet felt she could have done this forever. It was so tender yet also stirring in a loving fashion that made her stomach flip over with longing.

'I must go.'

Leif slowly released his arms and Juliet mischievously reached up to Leif's beard and gave it a gentle tug.

'And I love that too,' she said with a smile, and she turned and ran up the steps of the hotel.

Leif watched her disappear through the doors of the hotel before starting to make his way back to the campsite.

Tim Curley crept out of the shadows and began to follow Leif up the road. He stayed close to the hedgerows and despite his considerable bulk, moved silently and stealthily keeping a reasonable distance between his quarry and himself.

He followed Leif down the unmade road, past the Bush Retreat and watched him make his way to his tent, unlock it and crawl inside. Leif, filled with thoughts of Juliet, remained unaware of Curley's presence. Or of the malicious glint that filled Curley's eyes as he stared at the lone tent in the field.

23

'Darling, where on earth have you been?' demanded Sir Alec the moment Juliet entered the suite.

'Just for a walk,' Juliet replied, startled by her father's peevish tone. 'Why, what's the problem?'

His face softened. 'Sorry, you were out for such a long time. And I got worried. Worried in case you had had an accident.'

'Dad, I'm quite capable of looking after myself. You don't worry about me in London and that's surely way more dangerous than Scurra.'

Sir Alec laughed,' You're right. Put it down to old age. We just get more anxious.'

Juliet went over to him and gave him a hug and a kiss on the top of his balding head.

'Love you, Dad.'

'And I you, darling,' he said.

Edward, sitting by Sir Alec and with two paperbacks on his lap, one read and the other almost finished, looked up. 'I'm not surprised Alec worries – surely it's dark out there now?' he said.

'No, it's not too bad. I could see my way fine.'

'This holiday is doing you good, after all,' commented Sir Alec. 'There's a real glow about you. You really did look peaky this morning.'

Juliet smiled. She wasn't going to give away her reasons for the improvement in her looks. 'I do feel much, much better,' she agreed, and went to sit in the olive-green chair opposite her father and Edward. 'I thought tomorrow I would go for an all-day walk. I really want to concentrate on doing some sketches of the island.'

'Fine by me,' said Sir Alec, 'we have no plans.'

Edward nodded in agreement. 'Anywhere special in

mind?' he enquired.

'I'm not quite sure.' Juliet hesitated. 'Will you two be playing golf as usual?'

'We're both trying to reduce our handicap,' said Sir Alec wryly. 'I take it you wouldn't care to join us?'

Juliet shook her head. 'I'd only hold you up.'

Edward pointed to the Steelgate collection which Juliet had left on the coffee table.

'There's one of his paintings in the club house,' he said. He reached for the book and flicked through the pages. 'It's this one,' Edward turned the book round and held it up for Juliet to see.

It was in oils and was of the western side of the island, showing a field a mass of daisies, poppies and other wildflowers.

'It's near where the golf course is now,' commented Edward, and he continued to turn the pages, stopping at one depicting the Seven Stones. 'Now these really do intrigue me,' he said, looking at Juliet. 'And they're not too far away. I'll take you to see them tomorrow night. That can be your evening walk.'

'Thanks, but I've already been to see them. You'd be surprised at just how far they are,' Juliet replied.

'Then we'll drive to Lower Arch. They're not too far from there.' Edward closed the book and placed it back on the coffee table.

Sir Alec nodded his head approvingly. 'I think that's a good idea. And rather than dine here tomorrow night, why don't you two go off somewhere. A meal by candlelight, perhaps?'

'I don't think so,' said Juliet firmly. 'I'm quite happy to dine here with you, Dad.'

'As you please,' replied Sir Alec.

Juliet glanced at her watch and got up from the chair.

'Anyway,' she announced. 'I'm going to call it a day.' She retrieved the Steelgate book from the coffee table and kissed her father on his forehead. 'Good night, Dad,' she said.

'And no more silly dreams,' Sir Alec whispered. 'Good night.'

Juliet pointedly ignored Edward and went to her room.

Juliet sat on her bed and wrote up her diary. It had been a long day. Meeting Leif at Pear Beach, the coffee at Heaven's Drop Tea Garden, the visit to the market in the afternoon and the evening with Leif. She listed the events, wishing for once that the pages in her diary were longer.

When the entry was complete, she took a page from her writing pad and jotted down some words, carefully counting the syllables as she wrote. Her first attempt at *Leifu*. She would look again at what she had written in the morning and decide then whether to show them to Leif. She smiled with a gentle feeling of affection as she thought of his shyness at telling her about his unusual hobby. She slipped the paper in her diary and placed this on the Steelgate book.

She wondered if Leif was asleep yet or lying awake in his small tent. And what it would be like to sleep under canvas . . . what it would be like to be with Leif. She thought of him asleep, lying with his arms stretched out. Then called to mind his thick, unruly fair hair and the distinctive goatee beard and his smile. His warm, irresistible smile. She wondered if he had a girlfriend, either at university or at home. Had he ever had a lover? Did he feel for her as she was beginning to feel for him? He had looked at her so searchingly, so caringly – and those tender kisses. The mere thought of them made her melt. No one had ever kissed her in this almost magical way. Their eyes had met and lingered so often, as if they understood one another perfectly. At times there seemed no need for words.

Their eyebeams twisted and did thred each other on a double string . . . A sudden line of John Donne's poetry from her youth came to mind.

Juliet got up from her bed, quickly undressed and slipped on her nightshirt. She went to the curtains and looked out over the dark expanse of Hunter's Valley. She could see the lights of two farmsteads and the headlights of a car as it made its way down one of the twisty Scurra lanes. And she looked across to where the campsite was. It was now immersed in darkness and in the background loomed the unmistakable rise of the downs.

She heard voices outside the hotel and the distinctive cut-glass accent of Katherine Strevans. There were calls of *good night* and the slamming of a car door.

Juliet pulled back the curtains and turned. Edward stood facing her.

Juliet gasped in shock. 'I . . . I didn't hear you. Why the hell didn't you knock? I didn't invite you in.'

Edward stared back, taking in the contours of her body through her nightshirt. His eyes were misty, penetrating. Juliet edged back, pushing herself against the curtains, her arms shielding the top half of her body.

Edward moved towards her.

'What. . . what do you want?' Juliet demanded, alarm and fear coursing through her body.

'You,' he said.

'Get away, Edward,' she hissed. 'Don't come any closer. Stop hounding me. Make a move and I *will* scream the place down. I will!'

Edward stopped, his eyes fixed on her.

'If you're disturbed in the night,' he said. 'You know where I am. My bed is always waiting for you.'

Juliet looked back at Edward but said nothing.

'That's all,' he added, and he smiled. A smug, self-satisfied smile.

'I think I prefer the ghost,' said Juliet, 'Go away, Edward.'

Edward stayed where he was, still staring at Juliet.

'I want you,' he whispered.

Juliet shook her head.

'Some time soon,' he said. 'You *will* be mine.'

'Never, Edward. Never.' Juliet pressed herself further against the curtains and Edward backed away.

'Remember where I am, my dear,' he murmured. 'You may need me more than you think.'

Juliet watched as Edward stepped back and out of her room. As soon as he had gone, she rushed to the door closed and locked it. Then she turned and leant against the door, running her hands through her hair. She was angry and frightened. She had seen his look as he stared at her body through her nightclothes and she knew, more than ever, she had to keep him away. She'd have to talk to Dad, even if it did upset him.

Juliet took a deep breath before finally getting into bed and slipping under the duvet. The words of her father came to her. *No more silly dreams*, he had said. No. There would be no dreams, not tonight. And her anger at Edward gradually subsided as tiredness finally overcame her and she drifted off to sleep.

At 2.30 am, just after the clock on St Michael's had chimed, the tapping began.

Juliet stirred.

Tap.

Tap.

TAP.

At 3.10 the curtains began to move, just as if someone had brushed against them. And the room got colder. Markedly colder. Juliet wrapped the duvet tightly around her and slept on.

The curtains moved again, this time more wildly, as if someone had prodded them. Then all became still. All that could be heard was Juliet's soft breathing and the faint whir of the clock radio.

Ten minutes later she woke. She was cold and aware of something in her room. She lay still, her eyes wide and alert. There was no movement. No sound. And yet there had been something. . . something had disturbed her, of that she was sure. She thought of Edward. Had he tried to come in? . . . but, no, the door was locked.

She lay still for two, maybe, three minutes, watching wondering and listening. She glanced at the curtains. They were still, not like the previous night and there was now no tapping. It was just that her room was so cold, so uncomfortably cold and she somehow sensed the presence of another. Somewhere in the half-light someone, something lurked.

As the digits on her clock changed to 3:29 she acted. In one frantic movement, she kicked off the duvet, leapt out of bed and switched on the main light. And in the split second it had taken she heard a faint gasp. A gasp of surprise, the gasp of a young woman. And the vase containing the sweet peas suddenly teetered before crashing to the floor, the glass smashing into many tiny fragments, the flower water splashing Juliet.

'Who's there?' whispered Juliet, her body quaking with fear – and cold.

No response.

And as Juliet looked at spot from where the vase had fallen, she noticed that her diary had been moved and the book of Steelgate paintings had been opened – opened to the page that contained the painting of the Hunter family. The same painting that hung in the hotel lounge.

24

At half past seven, when most of the guests were still in bed and the kitchen staff were preparing breakfast, Juliet crept out of the Dickens Suite. Neither her father nor Edward had emerged from their rooms.

Upstairs all was quiet.

Juliet slipped down the two flights of stairs to the ground floor. Norman Strevans, always an early riser, was talking to a delivery man in the lobby. He nodded as Juliet passed him and watched as she went through to the lounge.

The curtains had already been drawn and one of the windows opened, but the room smelt stale from the night before. Someone had smoked several cigars and the ash and stubs still filled one of the ashtrays.

Juliet went across to the Steelgate paintings and gazed at the portrait of the Hunter family. All four of them looked back at her: the bearded man sitting proud and confident with his timid and shadowy wife beside him and their daughter, pretty and delicate, standing dutifully at her mother's side while her chubby and solemn brother was by his father. Steelgate had no doubt made the family appear as flattering as he could, but even so, he wasn't able to disguise the cold steel eyes of Mr Hunter.

Norman entered the room and approached Juliet.

'You're up early,' he said. He smiled as he spoke, hiding his concern at her early appearance. 'I hope you had no disturbance last night?'

Juliet continued to stare at the picture.

'Who were these people?' she asked.

Norman moved nearer and gazed at the painting himself.

'They're the Hunter family.'

'I know,' replied Juliet curtly. 'But who exactly

were they?'

He drew a deep breath. 'They were once an important family on Scurra. Their ancestry goes back many hundreds of years.'

'But these Hunters here,' said Juliet. 'Do you know anything about this group?'

He shook his head. 'Not much.'

Juliet looked across at him. '"Not much" means you know something. It is important you tell me.'

'Well,' the hotelier hesitated. 'Well, they were probably the last of this line of Hunters to live on Scurra. There was some scandal and I think Mr Hunter lost a lot of money speculating or gambling. The young lad, I believe, got killed in the Crimea.'

'And that young woman. What about her?'

Norman frowned. 'She was involved in a tragedy too.' He paused before adding, 'If you want to know more, I suggest you go to Narraport library. They have an excellent local history section.' The hotelier glanced at his watch. 'Anyway, if you'll excuse me, Miss Tyler.'

'Did they live here?' persisted Juliet.

'Pardon?'

'Here in this hotel? Did they live here?'

Norman Strevans pursed his lips and regarded Juliet thoughtfully. 'Yes. Yes, as a matter of fact they did.'

Juliet nodded. 'I thought so,' she replied. And as the hotelier withdrew from the lounge, she focussed her attention on the young woman standing by her mother. 'It's you,' she whispered. 'I'm sure it is. What is it you want?'

As the clock on St Michael's Church struck eight, Leif had already washed, dressed and eaten the yoghurt and orange he had kept for his breakfast. It was going to be another hot day and the tent, despite being cool overnight, was already becoming stuffy.

Leif locked his tent and set off to the Scurra General Stores. He posted the letter card to Agatha before entering the shop.

The aged shopkeeper, standing behind the counter, looked up.

'Morning,' said Leif brightly.

The old man grunted.

Leif went to the rack of postcards and selected three cards, two for university friends and the third, another sepia print, for his mother. He put the cards on the counter.

'Stamps?' asked the shopkeeper.

'Second class,' replied Leif.

The old man opened a red ledger by the till and took out a sheet of new commemorative stamps. He tore out three and Leif handed him the money.

'You the man at the campsite?' grunted the old man.

Leif nodded. 'I am. Why do you ask?'

'Just wondered.'

Leif looked at him inquiringly, wondering what was behind the shopkeeper's question. He pocketed the change and picked up the cards and stamps. 'You must have a reason for asking.'

'Just wondered.'

'Has Ma Demuth mentioned me?' Leif asked, remembering that Juliet had seen Ma at the shop the day before.

The old man's eyes narrowed.

'Has she? Because I need to know.'

The old man remained silent.

'Look, things have been happening.' continued Leif. 'Things I can't explain and I need to find out the reason.' Leif paused. 'So why did you ask if I was the man at the campsite? There are many staying at the campsite. Why me?'

'Because . . .'

'Because what?'

The old man took a deep breath.

'Tell me,' urged Leif. 'I need to know.'

''Tis the legacy.'

'The legacy?'

The old man nodded. 'It's come back.'

'What legacy?'

'Summat that happened a long time ago.'

'What?'

The old man shook his head. 'Best not spoke about.'

The shop door opened and a customer, the lady Leif had seen in the shop before, entered. She held a basket containing a spaniel. She went straight to the counter.

'Here you are, Steve,' she started, ignoring Leif. 'It's yours if you want it. Isn't he sweet?'

The dog barked and the shopkeeper lifted the flap of the carrier and bent down to examine it.

'You can tell me about the legacy later,' said Leif, but the old man's attention was now taken up by the dog.

Puzzled and perplexed, Leif left the shop and headed back to the campsite.

Edward Harrison picked up the phone and dialled a local number. After two rings a coarse voice answered.

'Well?' demanded Edward.

He listened and began to take notes. Not many, but they were enough.

A few minutes later he rang his secretary in London. Sandra was highly efficient and thorough, and he was confident she would deal with his instructions at once.

Fifteen minutes after leaving the shop, Leif arrived back at the campsite. He walked smartly across the field towards his tent.

'*Leif.*'

Leif spun round. The field was empty.

'*Leif.*'

Again he looked round, searching for the caller.

'*Leif.*' The voice seemed distant, almost echoey.

Leif turned again. And again. There was just no one there. And yet the voice had to come from somewhere.

Two rabbits hopped out from under a hedge and from their safe distance, stood and watched the bewildered young man.

Leif turned again – and it was then he saw. Hanging from the gibbet was a body encased in an iron cage. The body and cage seemed to quiver before, just like a dying rainbow, it faded from view.

25

Juliet ran to Leif's tent and pushed the flap aside. He looked up, smiled with sudden delight and backed out.

'Is anything the matter?' she demanded. 'You look a bit odd.'

Leif reached over and kissed her.

'And you look lovely,' he said, ignoring her remark.

'Has anything happened?'

'I'll tell you later. Like a drink before we go?'

Juliet shook her head. 'No. There's a taxi waiting.'

'Taxi?' queried Leif. 'What do we need a taxi for?'

'Dad and Edward have the car. Come on.'

Leif pulled up the zip of his tent, secured the padlock and slung his small rucksack over his shoulder. Hand in hand they quickly made their way to the yellow taxi waiting by the Bush Retreat. The driver, sporting a handlebar moustache, laid back in the driver's seat with his eyes shut.

'Is he all right to drive?' whispered Leif.

'Get in,' said Juliet giving Leif a nudge.

Leif opened the passenger door and they scrambled in. The driver sat up.

'You'll be lucky to make it now,' he grunted.

'They'll wait,' replied Juliet confidently.

The driver started the car up, revved the engine and drove at speed down the unmade road.

'Where are we going?' Leif asked.

Juliet smiled. 'To Bolt,' she answered. 'We've got all day. We're getting off this island.'

'You should have told me.'

'Why?'

'Because I'd have brought more money with me. For the fare and things.'

'Don't worry. This is my trip, my idea. I'll pay for

it.'

'I'd rather pay my share.'

She leant over and kissed him. 'No,' she said firmly and hesitated a moment. 'Leif, what's happened? When I arrived you looked as if you'd had some sort of fright.'

Leif took Juliet's hand. 'I've seen that image again.'

'At the gibbet?'

He nodded. 'It was a body in a cage and it was calling to me, actually calling my name. Then the image faded.'

'When was this?'

'About half an hour ago.' He hesitated. 'And there's another thing. Before that I went to the store and got talking to the shopkeeper. I said strange things had been happening and he mentioned something about a legacy. He didn't say what because another customer walked in. But I reckon he's been talking to Ma Demuth.'

'That wouldn't surpr—' Juliet broke off as the taxi swerved, overtook a tractor and hooted.

'Blooming berk,' shouted the taxi driver. 'These farmers think they own the road.'

'How about you?' Leif asked. 'Did you have a good night?'

'Not really.'

'Why? What happened?'

'I'll tell you in—' Juliet stopped again as the driver hooted and braked sharply, throwing both her and Leif forward. A blind man with his guide dog was walking across the road. The driver wound his window down and leant out.

'Everything all right, Charlie?' he called.

The blind man stopped. The dog turned and led Charlie to the side of the taxi.

'Oh, foine, Mr Russell. Thank you,' said the blind man. 'And you and Mrs Russell? Are you keeping well?'

'Busy,' declared the taxi driver.

"'Tis a busy time,' replied the blind man. 'All these 'olidaymakers. A good season, I gather.'

Juliet leant forward. 'We *do* have a boat to catch,' she reminded the driver.

'Be seeing you, Charlie,' The taxi driver waited for the blind man to move away before revving up again and hurtling down the roads towards the new Narraport harbour. They passed a policeman on a bicycle. The taxi driver hooted and waved. They were going too fast to notice the policeman's reaction.

'It's the Scurra Island Trips you want, love?' enquired the taxi driver.

Juliet reached in her pocket and took out the leaflet; the same leaflet she had used when she phoned to make the booking.

'Yes,' she replied.

They had reached the seafront now. On the one side were the numerous shops selling ice creams, gifts and quality clothes and on the other was the harbour full of yachts and small boats. Leif noticed several kiosks advertising fishing trips, trips to France, round the island, to the lighthouse and trips to Winderley and the uninhabited island of Bolt.

The driver waited for a break in the traffic before swinging the taxi across the road and pulling up by the red kiosk belonging to Scurra Island Trips. A weather-beaten sailor stood talking to a woman inside the kiosk.

Juliet and Leif got out of the taxi.

'I'll pay,' said Leif, reaching for his wallet.

Juliet shook her head and handed the driver a note, telling him to keep the change.

'Thanks, love,' the taxi driver said. 'Anytime you want a taxi, let us know. Russell's the name.' The driver revved the car and with a screech, sped off.

'Beats me how he keeps his licence.' The sailor

chuckled and looked across at Juliet. 'Are you the lady who phoned this morning?'

Juliet nodded.

'Well, here's your tickets.' The sailor reached over to the kiosk for two purple tickets and receipt and handed them to Juliet. 'Anyway,' he said. 'We're ready for the off,' and he led the way down some steps in the sea wall to a waiting open-topped launch. Some thirty tourists were on either side of the launch and they watched as Leif, Juliet and the sailor clambered on board.

Leif and Juliet headed to the front of the launch and sat on the slatted seats.

'We haven't kept them waiting for long, have we?' enquired Leif.

She shook her head and glanced at her watch. 'No. The boat's not meant to leave until 9.45. It's only 9:43. They're all early.'

The sailor positioned himself behind the wheel.

'Morning, ladies and gentlemen,' he began cheerily. 'Another fine day.'

Some of the passengers grinned, well pleased with the weather they were having for their holiday.

'My name's Tom and this is my son Andy.' Andy, a sturdy bronzed individual, nodded sheepishly and busied himself with the ropes. 'The sea's calm in the harbour, but it might get a bit choppy later. It will take about fifteen minutes to Winderley and we leave again at midday, at two o'clock and the last boat is at four. Don't miss the four o'clock boat or you may not get back.'

'I thought you said we were going to Bolt,' whispered Leif.

'We are.'

Tom started up the engine and soon the launch was pulling away from the sea wall and heading towards the mouth of the harbour.

Juliet shouted above the noise of the engine. 'This trip is to Winderley, but he does take visitors to Bolt as well.' She paused. 'According to local law, if it's not a private island or nature reserve, you can request to land on any island. And I requested to go to Bolt.'

'What's at Bolt?'

Juliet smiled and shrugged her shoulders.

'We'll have to see,' she said.

The launch cleared the protection of the harbour and almost immediately the sea became choppier. A wind whipped up some of the spray, blowing it back in the faces of those in the middle of the launch. Some of the holidaymakers reached for their jumpers or lowered themselves further in their seats for protection. Tom and Andy grinned.

'You get used to it,' Tom chuckled.

Leif put his arm round Juliet and they continued to look over the side of the boat, oblivious of the wind and spray. And before them lay a huge expanse of glistening sea dotted with some of the many rocky outcrops that surrounded Scurra.

Sir Alec placed his ball on the tee. It rolled off. He replaced it and again it rolled off.

'Damn thing!' he declared impatiently. He pressed the tee further into the ground and once more set the ball down. This time it stayed.

Edward watched the proceedings and waited for Sir Alec to take his shot. Sir Alec took his time. He was determined to reduce his handicap and had so far played well.

'A four iron, I think,' said Sir Alec thoughtfully.

Edward nodded and gazed across the course. Some other golfers that had set out ten minutes before them were no longer in view.

Sir Alec took a practice swing.

Edward looked at his watch and glanced out to sea. One of the Scurra ferries was leaving the island and a small launch was making its way on an island trip. At the front of the launch Edward could make out a young woman wearing a pale blue dress and a man in a white T-shirt with his arm round her.

'Alec,' said Edward slowly.

Sir Alec looked up.

'Is that Juliet?'

'*Juliet*? Where?' Sir Alec followed Edward's gaze to the small launch.

'In the blue dress,' added Edward.

Sir Alec squinted.

'It does look a bit like her,' he said, studying the small figures. 'But it can't be. She's out walking and besides, there's a man with her. No, can't be her.' Sir Alec turned his attention back to his shot while Edward continued to gaze at the figures on the launch. He had no doubt it was Juliet. The same hairstyle, the same colour outfit and she was with that man he had seen her with before. His eyes narrowed and hardened. This was definitely the secret of all her sudden disappearances.

The launch pulled away from Winderley leaving just Leif, Juliet, Tom and his son on board. Andy took the wheel and Tom made his way up the launch and sat opposite Juliet and Leif.

'So why Bolt?' he asked.

'I just fancied it,' said Juliet. 'I've always wanted to visit an uninhabited island.'

'Wasn't always like that. A hundred years ago they'd have been quite a community on Bolt. You can still see some of the houses.'

'Why did the people leave?' asked Leif.

Tom shrugged his shoulders. 'Better opportunities elsewhere. And the young went off to fight in the wars. Few returned. Mind you, one old dear, Betty Skirth, she would never leave. She lived alone on Bolt for well-nigh twenty years, until her final illness. Her old cottage is near the landing stage.'

Tom stretched his arms along the side of the launch and sighed. 'Lovely island though,' he murmured. 'Good place for bird spotting. Often see puffins.'

'Is that it?' asked Juliet, pointing to a hump-shaped island in front of them.

Tom nodded.

The sea ripped against some of the grey rocks surrounding the island and they watched as the launch passed many gaping caverns.

'It's flatter round the other side,' said Tom with a smile. 'And on the east side there's Bolt Pool. It's a large rock pool. Lovely for bathing.'

Andy manoeuvred the launch between an outcrop of rocks and then swung inland. The cliffs gave way to a small sandy beach and cobbled jetty. There was a shell of an old cottage at the far end of the beach.

'So here we are,' announced Tom some minutes later. 'An island to yourselves. There'll be no other visitors on Bolt today.'

They watched as Andy edged the launch to the old jetty. The steps were covered in seaweed and slime.

'Be careful,' warned Tom. 'We'll be back for you at three-thirty and because of the tides we'll pick you up from the next beach along. Okay?'

Leif nodded and helped Juliet off the launch and up the slippery steps. They stood hand in hand as they watched the launch pull away leaving them alone.

Slowly they made their way up the jetty and on to the warm and soft sand. Leif stopped and put his arms round

Juliet. 'This is going to be a lovely day,' he said softly. 'And we are going to forget all about Scurra. But, before we do, you didn't tell me about what happened last night.'

Juliet sighed. 'There was the usual drop in temperature and I vaguely remember hearing that tapping sound. Tap . . . tap . . . tap, just like that. As if someone was knocking at the window. And I sensed I was not alone, that someone else was in the room with me. I couldn't see anyone, but I leapt out of bed and turned the light on. As I did I heard the gasp of a woman and a vase containing some sweet peas crashed to the floor as if someone had knocked it.'

'And you're sure there was no one there?'

'Positive. And another thing, I have a book in my room. It's a book of paintings by a local artist called John Steelgate. When I went to bed the book was closed, but after I was disturbed I noticed it was opened. And it was open at a page showing a painting of the Hunter family.'

'Who are they?'

'They lived on Scurra a long time ago. And apparently at the hotel.' Juliet paused. 'There's this same painting in the lounge,' and she continued to tell Leif about what she had learnt from Norman Strevans.

'So, you think your room could be haunted by one of these Hunters?'

'I'm sure it is,' declared Juliet. 'By the young woman in the picture.'

'Why her?'

'Because I heard that gasp. And there's something about her – the way she stares out of the painting. And whenever I look at it – I mean at the original in the lounge – I somehow feel she's trying to reach out to me. I'm sure it's her.' Juliet paused and glanced over at Leif. 'You do believe me, don't you?'

Leif nodded. 'Of course, I do. We must believe each

other. And Juliet, I wish we knew what's going on. Why does it affect us so much?'

'I don't know. I don't know if I want to know. But anyway, let's forget all that for today. The sky is so blue, it's so peaceful and lovely here. Leif . . .'

And alone on a sandy beach on Bolt they held each other close and kissed.

Edward excused himself from the club bar, leaving Sir Alec talking to a Canadian visitor. He made his way to a side room and called a local number.

'Well?' he demanded on hearing Curley's coarse voice.

Curley grunted out the information he had found and Edward took the details.

'You've done well,' he said. 'I'll be in contact.'

Edward then dialled his London office and spoke to Sandra. She already had most of the information he had asked for and Sandra took down Edward's supplementary questions.

'I need this urgently,' snapped Edward and rang off.

He stayed in the room for a few more minutes and as he re-entered the bar, he watched Sir Alec laughing and nodding enthusiastically as he listened to the Canadian's escapades. All the same, he felt Sir Alec looked tired and ill and wondered how long the old man had left and whether Sir Alec regarded this holiday as his last.

Edward liked and admired Sir Alec. It had taken him several years to win his respect and confidence. All that remained was his daughter and soon . . . very soon, Juliet would be his. She would have no choice.

They climbed over rocks, ran down slopes, passed ruined cottages and watched rabbits play in long-abandoned gardens. They followed a track that ran across the island, passing large expanses of heather.

Near the middle of the island they came to the remains of an old chapel. The windows had been boarded up and a rusty padlock secured the large wooden door. Around the chapel were the crumbling graves of forgotten residents. A more recent grave, a granite tombstone, bore the name Betty Skirth, the last resident of Bolt.

Leif and Juliet made their way round the chapel. On the far side, set away from the other graves, was a granite cross. Old and weather-worn, the cross lent sharply to the left. A few winters more and it would be on its side.

'There's a painting of that in the Steelgate book,' said Juliet. 'It was upright then and had daffodils growing round it.'

Leif let go of Juliet's hand and made his way to the cross. On the centre the initials MEH were just visible.

'Songbird
alone on a tomb.
Respectful silence.'

'Leifu?'

Leif nodded. 'One I wrote some time ago. I've written quite a few,' he smiled. 'Come on, let's go.' And the two continued to make their way across the island, climbing more hillocks, pulling each other down grassy slopes and stopping to rest under the shade of a tree. Leif reached in his rucksack and pulled out a small packet of biscuits.

'This really is a lovely island,' he declared. 'An island of our own.'

Juliet turned to Leif and kissed his cheek. 'I wish this could last forever,' she murmured, 'I feel like a kid again.'

Leif tore the packet open and offered her a biscuit. They munched and drank from their water bottles, silent for a while.

'What do you think will happen?' she asked.

Leif sighed and leant back against the tree. 'To us?'

Juliet nodded. She remained sitting upright, stroking Leif's leg, gazing at the contours of his body. Leif closed his eyes, aware of the arousal caused by Juliet's sensual touch.

'You're not saying anything,' whispered Juliet.

'I'm thinking,' replied Leif.

'With every day
comes new possibilities.
See them. And seize them.'

'*Leifu*?'

Leif nodded and grinned.

'Then this is a piece of *Julietu*. Let's see if I can remember it.'

'Your presence. Your thoughts.
Your expressions. Your looks. All,
so uniquely you.'

'That's nice,' whispered Leif, and he reached over and kissed her in that slow, sensuous way that melted her inside.

At two thirty Edward was in his bedroom reading the notes he made after Sandra's latest call. He went over to the oval mirror that hung in his room, straightened his tie and brushed his thick waving brown hair. He smiled. He looked good and felt good. The sun and wind in Scurra had bronzed him nicely. He moistened his lips, took two deep breaths and went through to the main room of the suite.

Sir Alec was sitting on the settee with the *Daily Telegraph* spread in front of him.

'Alec,' Edward began. 'I've got some rather bad news . . .'

At the eastern tip of Bolt, they came to a grassy incline which gave way to gently sloping rocks and then to a wide expanse of beach. Juliet and Leif stood looking out to sea, which was a sparkling turquoise, darkened only by patches of seaweed and the rocks lying on the sandy bottom.

Hand in hand Juliet and Leif began to clamber down the slope and made their way down to the wide expanse of sand.

'I wonder if that's Bolt Pool?' said Leif, pointing to an area of water not far from where they were.

'Could be,' said Juliet and together they made their way to the edge of the pool. The smooth granite rocks had formed a large hollow and it was filled with glistening seawater. Although deep it was still possible to see the stones, pebbles and shells that lay at the bottom of the pool.

Juliet kicked off a shoe and dipped her toes in the water.

'It's lovely and warm,' she declared.

'Pity we didn't know about it,' said Leif. 'We could have bought our costumes.'

They stood for some moments gazing at the water. At last Leif turned and kissed Juliet on the neck.

'There's no one around,' he whispered.

Juliet looked back at him and he grinned playfully. She reached up and stroked his goatee beard.

'No,' she said thoughtfully. 'There is no one around.'

They kissed again and Leif pulled off his white T-shirt. Hesitating for just a moment, Juliet reached for the top button at the front of her dress. One by one she undid them, finally shrugging off the garment.

Leif watched her, marvelling at the beauty of her slender body. Now, she stood only in her underwear. She seemed almost shy, her eyes cast down. There was something so enticing about her modesty that he felt his heart swell with longing and love.

'Are you sure?' he asked.

She nodded, and he undid the bra, dropped the

garment and bent down to kiss her small erect nipples. As her body slowly, nervously responded to Leif's caresses, she ran her hands through his fair hair, kissing the nape of his neck. She became aware of Leif's fingers at the side of her pants and slowly felt them being slid down her slender legs. She stepped out of them and stood naked on the rocks of Bolt.

They kissed and caressed and she undid the zip on Leif's trousers. Soon Leif was out of his clothes and they stood locked in an embrace, tenderly exploring each other.

They settled on a large smooth rock, their bodies responding, touching. And with a long lingering kiss, Leif lowered himself on Juliet, pressing gently until he had entered her.

They lay still entwined for many moments. Then they swam and splashed in Bolt Pool, refreshed and revitalised by the cool clear water.

Several times they reached for each other and kissed.

'If only these moments could last,' whispered Juliet. 'I'm just so afraid.'

'Of Scurra?'

'Of Scurra. Of what's happening. Of . . . of the future.'

Leif smiled. 'Trust me. Please trust me, my love.'

Together they clambered out of the pool and lay on the smooth rock beside their bundle of clothes while the sun dried them. Then they made love again.

26

On her day off Ann Walker visited her aged parents at Parson's Cross. Although she had a small car, she preferred to walk, enjoying some of the back lanes of Scurra, lanes that only the locals and more adventurous tourists ever saw.

The hedgerows were colourful, the wildflowers emitting a sweet fragrance. The birds, unseen and high above her, sung their varied songs and Dizzy ran ahead of Ann, enjoying the freedom of the lane.

At Ripplebrook, a small thatched village featured in many postcards, Ann bought a choc ice and Dizzy enthusiastically lapped from a bowl of water outside the village store. Nearby Ann noticed Archie Cann dismantling the village pump, a job he was tackling without much enthusiasm.

'Morning, Annie,' he called, easing back his peaked cap. He was hot and his face was etched with lines of sweat and dirt. Dizzy broke off from his drink and ran to him. Ann followed.

'You've got some job there,' commented Ann, glancing at the many tools Archie had scattered around him. Archie wiped his forehead with an oily handkerchief.

'Only needs a damn good clean,' he sighed, stuffing the handkerchief back in his pocket. 'Not at the hotel today, then?'

'My day off.'

'Any more funny business?'

'Funny business?'

'Aye,' said Archie. 'In that posh suite upstairs?'

Ann looked inquiringly at Archie.

'Twice Strevans called me out,' he continued. 'Noisy pipes, rattling windows. Couldn't find nowt, though.'

'I didn't know anything about this,' said Ann slowly.

Archie nodded his head. 'Oh yeah. That posh girl made quite a fuss. And being who she is, like, they wanted it fixed.' Archie paused. 'But as I say, couldn't find nowt.'

Ann looked at him thoughtfully, recalling how only yesterday Cherie thought she had seen someone with her in Juliet's room.

'And you didn't find anything?'

'No,' said Archie dismissively. 'Nowt to find.' And he bent down and picked up an almost empty bottle of lemonade. 'You know these London sorts. Probably drank too much at the bar and had a nasty dream.' He paused as he took a swig. 'Mind you, Joe Sky won't go in that room. 'E says there's summat odd about it. But me, no.' Archie smiled. 'The man's daft. There's nowt wrong with it. Nowt at all.'

'I'm glad to hear that,' said Ann, and licking the rapidly melting choc ice, began to walk the remaining two miles to Parson's Cross. As she walked, the horrid coarse laugh of Ma Demuth returned to her and she recalled Ma's words in the park. *Things are 'appening. In 'er room upstairs.*

And Ann suddenly became fearful for that beautiful and wealthy young woman staying at the hotel.

Sir Alec left Edward at the hotel while he took the car to the northern end of the island and parked at a National Trust car park. He sat in the car for a while staring out at the scenery before setting off along the cliff walk.

He walked slowly, enjoying the warmth of the sun but preoccupied with his own thoughts. He had been disturbed by what Edward had told him and had no doubt Edward was right. Edward was always right.

He also knew that Edward was probably jealous, but

it was Juliet he was most concerned about. Above all he wanted her happiness and while he liked most of her friends none of them had, to his knowledge, criminal tendencies. None had been scavengers, befriending her just for her money. So far, he had been able to protect Juliet and it was his duty to protect her from this Olsen character. Whether by persuasion, law or some other means, he would prevent Olsen from ever seeing Juliet again.

Andy secured the launch on the old landing stage and with no sign of Juliet or Leif, the two seamen squatted on one of the large rocks on the beach.

'When I was a lad,' reminisced Tom. 'My dad often brought me here. We played on the beach and I remember Betty coming over and talking to us.'

'Wasn't she ever lonely?'

Tom shook his head.

'No. She loved Bolt. Was her home, it was. Her life.'

'Must have been difficult, all alone.'

Tom nodded. 'Daresay, but she never complained. She was always cheerful. And I'll tell you what, she was a darn sight happier than many folk on Scurra or the mainland.'

'Here they come,' said Andy, and he pointed to Juliet and Leif just appearing over a distant slope. They walked arm in arm, unaware of the arrival of the launch.

'You realise who she is, don't you?' asked Andy.

Tom shook his head.

'She's Juliet Tyler.'

Tom frowned.

'You know, Dad,' prompted Andy. 'Daughter of Sir Alec Tyler.'

Tom opened his mouth and let out a long whistle.

Andy smiled. 'Worth an absolute fortune, she is.

'Specially when the old man cops it.'

Tom nodded. 'Come to think of it, I did hear he was staying on Scurra.'

'At the Manor Hotel,' added Andy. 'And the chap with her is staying at the campsite.'

'You seem remarkably well informed,' Tom observed.

'Billy Bush told me. And,' he added, 'he's been telling a lot more besides.'

'Like what?'

Andy paused. Juliet and Leif had just seen them waiting and quickened their steps.

'Billy says Ma Demuth has been sniffing round.'

'Crazy old Ma?'

'That's right and, according to Billy, she came to the campsite and asked all about that man. Very strange she was. But she reckoned that even then things were happening between them.'

'How do you mean?'

'Between Miss Tyler and 'im. The chap staying at the campsite.'

'What if there is?'

'Well, Ma says, but she told Billy and Mrs Bush not to say anything, that it's to do with something that happened a long time ago. A sort of legacy, she said.'

Tom turned to his son and shook his head. 'I don't quite follow.'

Andy lent towards his father. 'Well, according to Ma, it's connected with a murder that happened a long time ago. She said that the person who did it still 'aunts the place.'

Tom chuckled. 'I really don't . . .'

'And,' continued Andy earnestly. 'Ma says that the murder 'appened in the very same room where Juliet Tyler is staying.' The young seaman paused as he watched Juliet and

Leif make their way across the sands. 'According to Ma, the woman murdered her lover. Stabbed 'im she did. Right through the heart.'

27

Tom assisted first Juliet in the launch and then Leif.

'Looks as if you had a fine time,' he observed.

They agreed.

'It's a lovely island,' added Juliet. 'So peaceful and quiet.'

'That it is,' said Tom, and he waited for them to get settled before starting the engine.

Juliet took hold of Leif's hand and gave it a gentle squeeze. 'I will never forget today,' she whispered.

Leif kissed Juliet on the cheek.

'Neither will I.'

The launch pulled away from Bolt and soon was ploughing its way past the rocks towards Winderley. Juliet and Leif looked back at the island, at its white sandy beaches, the dunes and desolate moorland beyond.

'One day I'll take you back,' promised Leif.

'Someday soon, I hope.' Juliet hesitated a moment and squeezed Leif's hand even tighter. 'I wish I was staying there with you. I just don't want to go back.'

'I'm not sure I do either.' Leif paused. 'Look, why don't you tell your father you can't stay in that room anymore. He'll understand, surely.'

Juliet smiled. 'You don't know my father. He'd think I was a coward or just being foolish.'

'But you must insist. I'm sure they can find you another room. I mean, I expect your father is paying a packet to stay there as it is.'

'I'll give it one more night. If anything happens, then I'll insist.'

'Well, remember, I'm not far away,' said Leif and he put his arm around her. 'And I needn't be far away. If I get my degree I will be working at Sibley's. And I can be in

London with you.'

Juliet rested her head on Leif's shoulder.

'I hope it will be the same,' she murmured.

'How do you mean?'

'With us. Life in London is so different from this.'

Leif stroked Juliet's hair thoughtfully.

'You go to a lot of functions, then?'

Juliet shook her head. 'Not really. Dad is always asking me, but I go to very few. I don't like them.' Juliet sighed. 'I hope it will be the same,' she repeated earnestly.

'It will,' replied Leif. 'I'll make sure it is.'

The launch stopped at Winderley and the holidaymakers, laden with carrier bags containing jumpers, sweatshirts and souvenirs from the island gift shop, struggled on board. An elderly couple, both sporting sunburnt noses, settled into the seats opposite Juliet and Leif.

As soon as the launch cast off, they began inspecting their purchases. The lady pulled out a sweatshirt containing a motif of a seagull perched on a rock and held it up against herself. Her husband said something complimentary. The woman looked across at Juliet and Leif.

'Ever so reasonable,' she started. 'Seconds – but couldn't find anything wrong with it.'

Juliet smiled politely.

'Arthur bought some fossils,' continued the lady. 'Go on, show them the fossils.'

The old man moved uncomfortably and muttered something under his breath.

'Well,' declared the lady impatiently. 'If you don't, I will.' The woman rummaged around and pulled out a paper bag, tipping the contents on her lap. There was a small historical guide to Winderley, two colourful pencils for their grandchildren and a fossil.

'Here it is,' she declared proudly. 'Millions of years

old it is and found on Winderley.'

The woman handed Leif the ammonite. It was a good specimen.

'Make a fine paperweight,' he commented.

Juliet glanced at Leif, not sure whether he was serious or joking. He handed the fossil back.

'Could I have a look at that guidebook?' he asked.

The elderly man passed the guide to him. It was a small publication titled *The History of Winderley* by Ralph de Montford. The guide was published by the Scurra Publishing Company.

Leif held the guide a moment without opening it.

'What are you thinking?' enquired Juliet.

'This reminds me of something,' he replied. 'At the Heaven's Drop Tea Gardens, they sold guides like this.' Leif turned the guide over and on the back was a list of other publications. 'Here they are,' he said. '*Walks on Scurra, Myths and Folklore of Scurra* and *Murders on Scurra.*' Leif glanced across at Juliet. 'When I first went to the tea gardens I looked at the murder book. There was something in it I read.'

'You didn't buy it?'

Leif shook his head. He now wished he had, but on his budget guide books, no matter how interesting, were a luxury.

'There's the Scurra rock,' shouted Tom from the back of the launch, and he pointed to a towering column of rock crowned by umpteen seabirds. As the majority on the launch hurriedly took photos, Juliet and Leif studied the guide.

As with the other guides, the print was small and the guide crammed with detail. The entire history of Winderley was covered, starting with a description of prehistoric finds, the arrival of early settlers, the several sieges, the famine of 1833 and a detailed account of Winderley during the wars.

There were also accounts of the famous who had visited the island, including visits by Queen Elizabeth I, King George III and the Princess Royal. There were the literary figures: Dickens, Tennyson and Wilkie Collins and the industrialists Isambard Kingdom Brunel and Andrew Squires. An engraving showed the latter, smiling and distinctive with the scar that ran across his right cheek. Another engraving showed The Cormorant, a large Victorian schooner, as she lay helpless on the rocks near Winderley.

Leif closed the guide book.

'You don't remember what you read?' asked Juliet.

'Not entirely. I mean I only glanced at it. But I did see a gory bit about someone who murdered lots of islanders and they tracked him down to a cave. And there was another about a murder at Hunter's Lodge.'

'That'll be the one,' declared Juliet. 'It must be. The hotel was owned by the Hunters. They had it for generations and it could easily have been called Hunter's Lodge.'

'In that case, we need to find out more about it. I tell you what, I'll go back to the tea gardens tomorrow and . . .' he paused and looked across at Juliet, '. . . no, let's both go along, shall we?'

Juliet nodded and gave him a kiss.

'Feeling any better now?' he asked.

She smiled and nestled against him and closed her eyes, relaxed by the rhythmic movement of the launch. And she thought of Bolt, of how she had given herself to Leif. She was usually so cautious with men, never a girl for one-night stands like so many of her friends who prided themselves in their conquests. It had happened so easily and naturally. She certainly had no regrets. She knew she was in love.

'We're almost here,' whispered Leif.

Juliet stirred and gazed up at the approaching harbour wall. Andy threw a rope to someone unseen above them.

'Well, I hope you all enjoyed the trip,' called out Tom, when the launch had been secured. 'It's round the island tomorrow if anyone's interested.'

The passengers, clutching their purchases and belongings, made their way slowly and unsteadily off the launch. Leif and Juliet were the last to leave.

'Good luck,' said Tom with a smile. 'Glad you enjoyed Bolt.'

'We did,' replied Leif as he assisted Juliet off the launch. Together they made their way up the damp steps. At the top stood Edward Harrison and Sir Alec Tyler.

'Dad!' Juliet started in shock and felt oddly guilty when she saw her father. 'I wasn't expecting . . .'

Her father looked at her sternly. 'Juliet, get in the car please.'

Leif let go off Juliet's hand, aware of Sir Alec and Harrison's gaze.

'What's wrong?' asked Juliet. 'Has anything happened?'

'Into the car,' ordered Sir Alec.

'I don't understand,' she protested. 'What's going on?'

'You'd better go,' whispered Leif. 'I'll see you later.'

Sir Alec held the car door open and reluctantly Juliet got in.

Edward Harrison approached Leif.

'Mr Olsen,' he began. He was much taller than Leif and dressed more for the city than a holiday island. 'Your presence is not wanted on Scurra. You're to get off the island tomorrow.'

Leif stared at Edward in disbelief. 'You must be—'

'If you do not,' cut in Edward. 'Things will get unpleasant, you understand?'

'Look,' said Leif. 'There's no—'

'You will of course be compensated,' continued Edward. 'When you leave the island a thousand pounds will be deposited in your bank account. And,' he added, 'given your pitiful state, I should imagine that would be very useful to you, wouldn't it?' He did not wait for an answer and turned to get in the car. 'We have your account number and details,' he added.

Leif reached forward and gripped Edward's arm. Edward Harrison pulled back sharply.

'If you think you can get me off Scurra, you can think again!' said Leif. 'Who the hell are you to order and bribe people like this? Juliet is an adult. It's her business who she wants to spend time with.'

Edward glared at Leif, his nostrils widening. 'I advise you to be sensible, Olsen. Otherwise life will become very difficult. And,' he added, 'you could find you haven't a job at Sibley's, after all. A job anywhere, come to that.' Edward turned, jumped in the car and almost before he had time to close the door, Sir Alec pulled the car sharply away.

'You bastard!' shouted Leif, and he watched as the Rolls merged in with the holiday traffic. The last he saw was a fleeting glimpse of a sobbing Juliet sitting beside her father.

28

As soon as Sir Alec, Juliet and Edward arrived back at the hotel, Edward stormed over to the reception desk.

'Yes, Mr Harrison?' enquired Jill with a fixed but courteous smile.

'Mr Strevans, please.'

Jill gave a nod of her head and withdrew to the office behind her. She was relieved Harrison did not want to speak with her. He was cold, austere and not the sort Jill liked dealing with.

'Mr Harrison would like to see you,' she announced.

Norman looked up from the crossword he had almost completed. He gave an exasperated grunt, eased himself out of his swivel chair and went through to the desk.

'Yes, Mr Harrison?' he asked. 'What can I do for you?'

'Miss Tyler is being pestered by some student here on holiday. The fellow's uncouth and unwelcome. His name is Olsen and can be recognised by a short and ridiculous beard. If he enters this hotel he's to be ejected immediately. Is that understood?'

'Well, I can't really prevent him if he enters peacefully for a drink or whatever . . .' Norman said dubiously.

'In that case, if you consider yourself so incapable of action, send for me and I'll dispatch him, don't you worry. The onus will be on me.'

Norman Strevans nodded.

'And should anybody phone for Miss Tyler they are to be informed she's not available. I presume you can manage that much?'

'Anyone?' queried Norman, wisely ignoring the

jibes. 'Male or female?'

'Anyone,' snapped Edward. 'Olsen will be leaving Scurra tomorrow but he may try to contact Miss Tyler in the meantime.'

'I'll see to it that he doesn't. Leave it with me.'

'Good.' Edward looked hard at the hotelier, leaving him in no doubt about the seriousness of his instruction.

'And you'll inform your staff, you understand?'

'Of course,' replied Norman. 'You may rest assured Miss Tyler will not be disturbed.'

'Good.' Edward Harrison gave a nod of satisfaction, turned abruptly and headed towards the stairs.

'Silly sod,' muttered the hotelier under his breath. He looked over to Jill. 'You heard all that?' he asked.

The receptionist nodded. 'Horrible man,' she agreed, 'Shall I tell the others?'

'You'd better. I'll tell the wife. Just hope she doesn't start erecting barricades.'

Upstairs, Sir Alec took Juliet's hand.

'Darling,' he said consolingly. 'You must realise you are all I have. And I want your happiness.'

Juliet sat motionless, her gaze fixed upon the mottled carpet.

'I don't usually interfere in what you do,' Sir Alec continued. 'But I do have to protect you, you understand?'

Juliet's eyes swelled with tears.

'You are a rich woman and there are plenty who will try to befriend you for your money. And that man Olsen is not worthy of you. He has no job, no money, no prospects.'

'He has an offer from a publisher. He will have some work,' Juliet retorted.

Sir Alec smiled sympathetically and shook his head. 'That was just a vague promise. It's unlikely to ever come to anything.'

'How do you know?'

Sir Alec took a deep breath. 'Because we checked.'

'*We*?' asked Juliet, turning sharply towards her father, her face distorted with anger. 'It was Edward, wasn't it? Wasn't it?'

Her father stared at her, surprised at her fury. She was usually such a docile girl, always ready to take his paternal advice. He'd had to be mother and father to her – who else could guide her in these matters?

'Yes, it was Edward. But he always has your . . . and my . . . welfare at heart. When he found out you were seeing Olsen, he made enquiries. He cares for you as much as I do.' Sir Alec paused. 'We have to check all the time. We have to be so careful. It's not as if you are just an ordinary girl. And if this Olsen had been a respectable individual, you would have been none the wiser about our enquiries.'

'But he *is* respectable,' protested Juliet.

'My dear, whatever Olsen has told you, he's a liar. He's no good and he's just after your money. He has a criminal record and, if you must know, has lived with some woman in Bournemouth for the last three years.'

'I don't believe it,' gasped Juliet. 'I just don't.'

'You're going to have to. We have the proof. The woman's name is Barbara Anstey and, as for this matter with the police, it's—'

'Edward has made all this up,' cut in Juliet. 'It's just not true.'

'It's true enough,' said Sir Alec firmly. He let go of Juliet's hand, eased himself up from the settee and went over to the mantlepiece. He ran his eye over the collection of brass miniatures adorning it. 'Yes, it was Edward who drew my attention to Olsen. And I'm glad he did. Edward is a man of integrity and loyalty.' Sir Alec turned and faced his daughter. 'Juliet,' he said. 'You are a woman with responsibilities. You need to grow up. Forget this holiday romance.'

Juliet bit her lip and without saying anything, got up and went to her room, slamming the door behind her.

Leif strode along the seafront, seething at the turn of events. From the moment he had seen Edward Harrison on the ferry he had taken a dislike to him. He should have realised before that Harrison posed a threat. But not like this. Not by bribery and by wrecking his prospects at Sibley's.

He was puzzled how Harrison had found out about his job and wondered what else he'd discovered. That man was an impossible bully. Who did he think he was? Juliet was a grown woman, not a child. He had to see Juliet again and put her mind at rest.

From the harbour, Leif headed towards the centre of Narraport. He bought a can of Coke from a kiosk and, just as he was about to open it, a red open-topped bus pulled up at a nearby stop. It was the 29, the bus that took the coastal route round the island – a route that would take it close to Heaven's Drop. Leif joined the queue and hoped that by the time the bus had negotiated the holiday traffic he would still find the tea gardens open.

The journey took twenty minutes. Leif got off at Heaven's Drop car park and ran the short distance to the tea gardens. The sign advertising Scurra Ice Cream was still up and a battered orange mini was parked outside.

Leif pushed the gate open and went around to the back of the garden. He glanced at the red-hot pokers and the roses that Juliet had so much admired, then at the table where they had sat and which still had the remains of someone's cream tea.

The back door of the cottage was open and hanging on the door was the rack of postcards and booklets. Leif started to flick through them when Frankie, wearing an apron with I'M YOURS emblazoned on the front, came out from the kitchen.

'I'm dreadfully sorry,' he started. 'We're closed.' He looked hot and flustered.

'I just wanted a booklet,' replied Leif.

'It's been such a day. Just hasn't stopped.' Frankie paused. 'So which booklet is it you want?'

Leif continued to study the books on the rack. 'It's the murder booklet,' he said.

Frankie gave a cursory look at the rack.

'I'm pretty sure that one's gone,' he declared. 'Some Yorkshire people bought it. And the one on the ruins of Scurra.'

'Do you have any more copies?' enquired Leif, checking the last of the booklets.

'I can look,' Frankie said and withdrew into the cottage and into the dark living room. Leif followed. The room was sparsely furnished and a threadbare carpet covered the stone floor. Little would have changed over the last hundred years.

Frankie took a small brown box bearing the insignia of the Scurra Publishing Company from the oak sideboard and placed it on the table. He lifted the flaps and went through the packet of booklets in the box.

'No,' he said at last. 'Only the rambling, motoring guides and local recipes left.'

'Well, thanks for checking,' sighed Leif.

Frankie folded the flaps back over the box.

'It was just the murder booklet you wanted, was it?'

'Or on Scurra ghosts, if they did one.'

'Any reason?'

'I'm interested in a murder committed at Scurra Manor Hotel.'

Frankie looked at Leif. 'Now that was some murder,' he said with satisfaction.

'You know about it?'

'As much as most islanders know.'

'Then tell me. It's important.'

Frankie pulled a chair from the table and settled himself opposite where Leif was standing.

'Happened many years ago,' he started. 'In the 1830s. The girl who lived at the hotel, Mary Hunter I believe her name was, stabbed her lover. He was a local lad and she was hung.' Frankie paused. 'Nasty business, it was. It was made all the worse because she came from a respected family. Lived on Scurra for centuries they had and then this happens. But despite their wealth and prestige, they couldn't stop the hanging. The family left Scurra soon after and never returned. And,' Frankie added, 'I've heard it said that Mary Hunter haunts the place where she lived.'

'The Scurra Manor Hotel?'

Frankie nodded.

'Except it wasn't called that then. Some guests have seen her ghost wandering about, apparently looking for her lover. It's not common knowledge, but a ghost-hunter stayed at the hotel once though I'm not sure he found anything. Of course, the Strevans try to ignore it. I mean it wouldn't be good publicity, would it?'

'How many have seen the ghost?'

Frankie shook his head. 'As a matter of fact, very few. But those that have seen it, well . . .' Frankie trailed off.

'Well what?'

'Well, it's because the ghost seemed to want to contact them.'

'How do you mean?' asked Leif.

Frankie leant forward in his chair. 'It's usually young women who see her. Miserable, sad women, like the ghost herself.'

'And does anything ever happen after they've seen the ghost?'

Frankie shrugged his shoulders. 'Don't know,' he

replied. 'If it does, no one has ever told me.'

29

The phone rang. Katherine Strevans emerged from the dining room and hurried across to answer it, annoyed that Jill was not there.

'Could you please put me through to Miss Tyler,' asked Leif.

Katherine stiffened. Norman had warned her not to accept calls for Miss Tyler but she had not expected one so soon.

'Miss Tyler is unavailable,' she replied curtly.

'It's extremely important,' insisted Leif.

'Miss Tyler is unavailable,' she repeated and put the receiver down.

Almost immediately the phone rang again.

Katherine picked up the receiver once more as Jill returned to the desk.

'Scurra Manor Hotel,' Katherine answered.

Silence.

'Hallo?' enquired Katherine. 'Scurra Manor Hotel. Can I help you?'

'Mrs Strevans,' came a harsh voice.

'Yes.'

'Ma here.'

More silence and Katherine shot a none-too-pleased glance in Jill's direction.

'Yes?'

There was no reply, just the sound of Ma's breathing.

'Is there something you want, Ma?' asked Katherine impatiently.

'There is,' replied Ma. 'I've seen Mary Hunter.'

'Mary Hunter. But . . .' Katherine's voice trailed off.

'That's right. She's come back.'

The phone clicked as Ma Demuth replaced the receiver. Katherine stood still for a few moments before she too put the phone down.

'Is anything wrong?' enquired Jill.

'No,' said Katherine. 'No!' And she hurried out of the reception in search of Norman.

After Leif had been rebuffed by Katherine Strevans, he phoned home. There was still no answer. His mother should have been there – unless she was seeing David. He would leave it another day. If there was still no answer he would contact a neighbour to make sure everything was all right. He felt hounded and afraid for everyone connected with him.

Leif left the phone box and continued to make his way back to the campsite. Several times he tried for a lift, but no one stopped. He walked through Lower Arch, passing the alleyway he had taken on his walk to the Seven Stones. Sometimes he glanced up at the gibbet. And he thought of the time he had met Juliet up there and how he had given her a drink. And he thought of Bolt. Of the lovely time they had spent there. It had been so perfect, such loving, tender moments. And now it seemed so different. Juliet had been snatched from him and his future threatened. But the threats made no difference. If it meant losing his job, he would get another. Maybe an even better job. Anything, but he would get Juliet back too, of that he was determined.

Leif passed the Compass. Mainwaring was outside, noisily rolling a barrel round to the back. When he saw Leif, he stopped.

'Darts match tonight,' he declared cheerily. 'Should be a good 'un. Us against the Fox.'

'Hope you win,' Leif called back and continued on his way, coming at last to the unmade road. He passed the Bush Retreat – Billy Bush was loading some amplifiers in the back of a dusty Ford van – passed the fields containing the other campers, and on to the field containing his lone tent.

He saw it almost immediately. The zip on his tent door was half undone – someone had removed the padlock and been into his tent. That explained how Harrison had found out about his job offer. Warily, he approached the tent and pushed back the flap. There was no one in it, but someone had riffled through his belongings. The bags containing his possessions had been emptied and the rucksack containing his papers had been scattered over the floor. His book of *Leifu*, his address book, notepad, unwritten postcards, the paperback he was reading, had all been tipped out. And the loose letters that had been tucked inside his diary – including a letter from Sibley's – had been taken out and no doubt read.

Leif checked under the sweatshirt he had been using as a pillow. His remaining money was still there. Nothing had been removed from the tent – only information.

'Leif?' A voice called urgently.

Leif spun round.

'Leif. Are you there?'

He crawled out of the tent to find Rose Bush hovering above him. She looked agitated.

'Oh, thank goodness,' she said on seeing him. 'I've been so worried.'

'Someone's been in my tent,' Leif declared.

Rose nodded, her chubby face twitchy and anxious. 'Stephen Moss saw someone. He's one of Mr Robson's boys. He said he saw someone at your tent. When Thomas came to look he had gone. They just left your tent undone and the padlock broken. Leif, is anything missing?'

He shook his head.

'We think,' said Rose cautiously, 'it might be Tim Curley. He was seen hanging about the site last night.'

'And who is Tim Curley?'

'A most unpleasant piece of work. Been inside, you know.' Rose paused. 'Rotten to the core. The strange thing is he has such a nice mother.'

'What does he look like?'

'Grotesque. That's the only way to describe him. Fat, deep set eyes and a boxer's sort of nose. You can't mistake him. But as to why he should do this, I just don't know.' Rose hesitated. 'Still, if you say there's nothing missing, that's the main thing, and Thomas will give you another padlock. He has several.'

'And one that's Curley-proof,' added Leif.

Rose turned to go and then hesitated, looking back at him. 'Oh, I almost forgot. An Agatha Hickstead phoned for you. She was most anxious to find out if you were all right. And she asked me to tell you to be careful. She kept saying it over and over again. Tell Leif to be careful. It was . . . well, her whole manner was most strange.'

He smiled. 'Agatha's my aunt,' he explained. 'And she does tend to worry a lot.'

'Well she's certainly worrying about you now. But Leif, you will be careful, won't you?'

'Of course. I always am.'

Rose Bush took one more look at Leif before slowly beginning her way back across the field.

He gave a long and weary sigh. Agatha had an aversion to the phone and for her to have contacted the campsite must have taken a supreme effort. She must have had another of her visions. And her visions rarely let her down.

30

Juliet sat on the edge of her bed with her sketch pad resting on her lap. She turned to a clean page, her mind filled with the images of the day.

Idly she drew a line, then another, gradually letting the drawing take shape. There was a column. A leaning column. Crooked and gnarled. She added another piece, turning the column into a cross, then into the gravestone she saw on Bolt.

She sketched in the vague outline of the chapel in the background, and of the moors. Then she filled in more detail of the grave: the staining and decay caused by years of neglect, and at the centre of the cross she pencilled in the initials MEH.

She laid her pencil down.

'Mary Hunter.' she whispered. 'Mary E. Hunter.'

Juliet gazed at the drawing, raised it to her lips and kissed the cross. 'If it's you,' she said softly. 'Please help.'

It was too hot for his guernsey, but Leif slipped it on. It was the smartest top he had. And he put on his beige cotton trousers – not that they matched, but they were the most presentable trousers he had left. He brushed his hair, checked his appearance and set off for the Scurra Manor Hotel.

He saw the emerald Rolls parked in the car park, along with some other grand and expensive cars. Several residents, already dressed for dinner, stood on the steps chatting and laughing. They gave Leif a superior look as he passed and entered the hotel.

Jill noticed him as soon as he entered the lobby and pressed the buzzer under the desk, inaudible to residents, but alerting anyone in the office or downstairs of a problem.

Leif approached the desk, smiling nervously.

'I was wondering if I could see Miss Tyler for a moment?'

'I'm afraid it is not possible,' Jill replied, hoping someone would come quickly.

'Just a quick word,' He nodded towards the phone on the desk. 'You could call her room. Or I could.'

Jill shook her head. 'I'm sorry. I have . . .' she trailed off as Norman Strevans appeared. Leif turned and watched as the proprietor headed towards him.

'This gentleman is asking for Miss Tyler.'

Norman looked at Leif firmly.

'Miss Tyler is seeing no one at present. Would you please leave the hotel.'

'Can I leave a message?' asked Leif.

'No. Now would you please leave.'

'Just a short—?'

'Get out.'

Leif bristled. Although much slighter than the hotelier, and no match for Strevans, Leif remained where he was. 'I want to leave a message for Miss Tyler,' he insisted.

Norman Strevans advanced towards him. 'Get out of my hotel or I'll call the police.'

'Do that,' said Leif, 'I'm hardly breaking the law, am I? I might want a word with them myself. Why is Miss Tyler being kept a prisoner? That's what it amounts to.'

Norman nodded towards Jill and Jill reached for the phone.

'But if you give a message to Miss Tyler I will leave. And leave without causing a scene.'

Norman's whole manner became more agitated.

'Out,' he ordered.

Leif smiled, shook his head and folded his arms defiantly. 'Not until I have given a message to Miss Tyler.'

At that moment Edward Harrison came down the stairs. He took one look at Leif before starting towards him.

'Get him out,' he snapped.

Norman made a grab for Leif's arm, but Leif pulled back. Together Edward and Norman advanced. Leif moved back a step. Then, with a deft movement, Norman lurched forward, grabbing Leif's guernsey. Leif struggled. Harrison, taller than Leif, grabbed his arm and the two pushed and propelled the young man out of the lobby and down the steps. Once at the bottom, Harrison pushed Leif who fell back on the gravel. As he struggled to his feet, Harrison pushed him back again and knelt down so that he was close to Leif.

'Be off this island tomorrow,' warned Edward. 'Or you will regret it? Understand?'

Leif kicked out, almost causing Edward to lose his balance. Edward glared, stood up and withdrew into the hotel with Norman Strevans following closely behind.

Upstairs, Sir Alec gazed out of his window at the dishevelled and angry figure sprawled on the gravel. And a hint of a smile appeared as he watched Leif indignantly get to his feet.

Juliet removed the last of her clothes and looked down at her slender body. The body she had given to Leif that afternoon. She would never forget their lovemaking, or the lovely pool at Bolt.

She wondered if her father had been telling her the truth. Was it true that Leif had lived with another woman, had a police record and dubious background? Her father would not lie, and yet Leif seemed so sincere, so genuine and so unlike anyone she had ever met.

She heard someone at the door. Damn, she'd forgotten to lock it and there could only be one person rude enough to barge unasked into a woman's room. Swiftly she grabbed her nightshirt and held it against her, shielding her body. The door opened and Edward entered. He had already changed for bed and wore blue and white striped pyjamas and a mauve dressing gown. He smiled as he observed Juliet's state of undress. Juliet held the skimpy garment tightly around herself.

Edward moved towards her.

'Get out,' snapped Juliet, aware of her vulnerability.

Edward gazed at her with longing eyes and slowly advanced. Juliet took a step back, feeling the curtains against her naked back. Still he came forward until he stood in front of her. He smiled, leaned over and kissed her.

Juliet pulled her head away. 'No,' she gasped.

He kissed her again, this time on the cheek, and then placed his hands upon her bare shoulders. She kept the nightshirt firmly pressed against her.

'I love you, I want you,' whispered Edward. 'Come on, Juliet, stop playing so hard to get.'

Juliet said nothing.

'You can't resist forever. You need me as much as I need you.'

Juliet stared at him, her eyes wide, angry and afraid.

'You must put that other man out of your head,' he said quietly, his hands squeezing her shoulders. 'He's poor and far too young. You need a mature, sensible man in your life.'

'Who are you to judge what I need, Edward Harrison,' she said angrily. 'You mean *nothing* to me.'

'He was after your money, Juliet. You need protection. Love.' Edward leant forward and kissed her on the lips. He pressed hard and felt her sharp intake of breath as his hands reached for the nightshirt she held against her. Juliet's grip tightened.

'Edward! Just go away and leave me alone!'

Edward still had a hold of her nightshirt and pulled at it, his eyes fixed on Juliet.

'No!'

He gave a tug, partly exposing Juliet's breasts.

Juliet pulled her nightshirt back.

'Get out,' warned Juliet. 'Dad!' she shouted. 'Dad!'

Edward immediately released his grip on the material and put a hand over her mouth. 'He won't have heard that, my dear. Not with his medication.'

She pulled her head away from his restricting hand.

'Get *out*!' she repeated. If there had been some heavy object close by she would have hit him with it and to hell with the consequences. He saw her eyes looking around and seemed to guess her thought.

'My sweet little wildcat,' he murmured, 'I'm going to have you in the end. I'm going to have you, Juliet. You'll have no choice.' Edward took one more look at her before moving back towards the door.

She waited for him to leave the room before she finally slipped into her nightwear and locked the door with a sigh of relief.

At half past eleven much of the hotel was in darkness. Only the lights from the lobby, the bar and several of the upstairs rooms were on.

For several minutes Leif stayed crouched behind one of the large bushes in the grounds. There was little movement or sound. Only the occasional hoot of an owl or distant car.

Leif noticed the security lights positioned around the hotel and which would emit a powerful light as soon as anyone crossed the beam. He studied the lights for several moments, deciding how best to avoid detection. Juliet's room was in darkness, her curtains drawn, windows firmly shut. Had there been a drainpipe he would have tried to climb up. But there were no drainpipes or any obvious way up.

Leif edged his way round the bush and crept

forward, his feet silent on the short, parched grass. Just yards from the hotel he stopped, bent down and picked up several small stones from one of the flower borders. He positioned himself under the window, took one of the stones and aimed it at Juliet's window. The stone hit the wall just below her window before rebounding back on the gravel path.

As he took another stone, there was a momentary flutter and a small bat brushed against him. Startled, he jerked back, making sure the creature had gone.

He threw another stone. This hit Juliet's window, chinking as it touched the glass before falling back. Leif waited, hoping Juliet had heard. There was no response. He threw another, this time landing just above her window. The next stone hit, but again there was no response.

Leif took aim with a fifth stone and just as he prepared to throw, a hand yanked him back.

''Ere, what's your game?'

Leif spun round. The man, about Leif's age and with short cropped hair, glared at him.

'I was trying to contact someone.'

'Oh yeah?'

Leif took a chance. 'Do you live here?' he asked.

'What if I do?'

'Could you give a message to someone? It's really important.'

The man regarded Leif warily.

'A girl, is it?'

Leif nodded.

The man stared at Leif. He too was aware of the passions of love.

'If you get going.'

'I will if you give her a message.'

'I'll see what I can do,' replied the man.

Leif reached in his trouser pocket and took out a pen and the only scrap of paper he had, an old till receipt. He scrawled a short message on the blank side of the receipt, folded it up and handed it to the man together with a fifty pence piece, all he had in his pocket.

'It's for Juliet Tyler,' he said.

The man took the paper and coin, slipping it in the wallet in his back pocket.

'You promise you'll give it to her?'

'If I can,' replied the man. 'Now get going.' And he watched as Leif withdrew into the darkness of the Scurra night.

'You know something, Paul,' declared Jill as they lay exhausted in bed. 'You're naughty but nice.'

Paul sniggered and kissed Jill.

'So are you,' he replied. 'Leading me astray like this.'

The two lovers kissed again and Jill, who was on top, eased herself off Paul. They lay in bed gazing up at the ceiling.

'I wonder if Strevans and his wife still do it?' said Paul with a grin.

'Do what?'

'Make love.' Paul smiled and glanced over at Jill.

Jill giggled. 'What a thought.' She hesitated. 'Mind you, I did hear Norman had an affair with someone a long time ago.'

Paul sighed contentedly, staring at the ceiling.

'Funny thing, love,' he murmured. 'Tonight, I caught a chap throwing stones at his girlfriend's window.'

Jill looked over at her lover. 'What, here?'

Paul nodded. 'In the grounds. He was just standing there throwing stones.'

'It wasn't a chap with a goatee beard, was it?'

Paul thought back a moment.

'Yes. Why?'

'He's been pestering Juliet Tyler. We've been warned against him,' Jill smiled. 'In fact, Norman and Mr Harrison threw him out of the hotel tonight. They got really physical they did.'

'No one told me. Anyway, he gave me a message to give to her.'

'Really?'

Paul nodded.

'And will you?'

Paul smiled, flicked on the bedside light and retrieved his wallet from his discarded trousers. He took out the piece of paper Leif had given him, read it and shoved it back in his wallet.

'What does it say?' Jill asked, leaning over Paul.

'It's private.'

'Let me see?' Jill begged.

Paul switched off the light.

'Good night.'

'What does it say?' whispered Jill, pressing her naked body against his, her hands wandering over his chest. 'What does it say?'

'It's private,' teased Paul.

They kissed.

'Will you give it to her?'

'I'll think about it,' he said, and he pulled Jill closer.

31

It was a still night. The moon was full, the air cool and Leif was unable to sleep. His mind was a whirl with the events of the day, of his time with Juliet and then his two confrontations with Edward Harrison. He knew more than ever that he had to see Juliet and put her mind at rest. The last time he had seen her, she was crying and grief-stricken. Whatever her father had said had greatly upset her. And he prayed the man he had met in the hotel grounds would give her his note.

Leif looked at his watch and in the half-light was just able to make out it was some time after one. He closed his eyes.

He heard the clock on St Michael's Church strike four. At five it was light. Fitfully he dozed and at seven he pulled up the zip on his tent and gazed out. A vale of mist hung over the field and high above the gibbet stood proud, silhouetted against the hazy sky.

Slipping on his clothes, he crawled out of the tent and set up his camping stove to boil some water. He retrieved the matches from the inside pocket of the tent and struck one. No sooner was it alight than the flame died. He struck a second.

'*Leif.*'

Leif turned, the match still alight in his hand.

'*Leif.*'

The voice was of a young woman, echoey and faint.

'*Leif.*'

He turned, his eyes falling upon the gibbet. And there, suspended from a noose, was a female figure dressed in a dowdy brown. This time the body was not in a cage.

'*Leif,*' the voice called again.

Leif stared, transfixed by what he saw. The flame from the match singed the tips of his finger. He shook the match, extinguishing the flame and looked back at the figure. She was still there and her right arm began to reach out, as if beckoning to him.

Slowly, hesitatingly, Leif started to make his way towards the path that led to the downs and the gibbet.

Juliet slept on through the night. There had been no knocking, no sudden drop in temperature or shaking of curtains. And as it got light she vaguely heard sounds of a milk float as it rattled up the drive.

She yawned and stretched. The sun filtered through the chinks in the curtains casting patterns on the floral carpet. It was going to be another fine day.

She turned over and dozed.

It was a jolt that woke her. Someone was shaking her, rousing her.

'All right. All right,' she protested.

She yawned again and felt a weight pressing down on her bed, as if someone was now sitting on the edge of it.

'I'll get up,' she murmured. Sleepily she glanced at the clock on her bedside cabinet. It was 8:48. She turned over. The weight on her bed lifted off and she looked up.

There was no one there. And then she remembered the door. After Edward had left the room last night she had locked the door and the key still lay on her dressing table, exactly where she had left it.

Puzzled, alarmed, she swung herself out of bed and tried the door. It was still locked. No one could possibly have got in. Warily she moved back to the bed, sitting on the edge. 'Mary,' she whispered. 'Mary, is that you?'

Juliet remained still. Watching, listening and aware her room had started to get colder.

'I know you're here,' she said softly, her eyes

darting about the room. 'What is it you want?'

Still she watched. And listened.

There was a creak. Or was it a gurgle in one of the water pipes? Noise from a radio filtered through to her bedroom and she could hear her father say something to Edward.

'You must tell me,' Juliet insisted.

She heard movement outside her door.

'Juliet,' her father called. 'Are you up?'

'Yes,' she replied.

'It's almost breakfast time.'

'I'll be through shortly.' She waited for her father to move away. 'What do you want?' she asked again.

Still there was nothing.

Getting off her bed, she went across to her wardrobe and pulled out the white cotton blouse from off a hanger and her patterned skirt. The skirt had got slightly creased on the journey and Juliet brushed it, trying to smooth it out. It was only then that she noticed the curtains in her room were quivering, just as if someone had brushed lightly against them. Warily, silently, she moved across to them.

'Mary,' she whispered.

There was no reply. Just a gentle buffeting of the material.

'Mary, is that you?'

Juliet watched. Still the curtains moved. Then, in a split second, she lunged forward, pulling the curtains apart. There was a gasp, like the one she had heard before, and she saw the faint image of a young woman. The woman had her back to her and had long flowing black hair trailing onto a grubby brown tunic. Juliet watched incredulously as the image faded from view. And was no more.

Leif crossed a stile at the end of the field and started up the steep ascent of Gibbet Hill. Sometimes the gibbet was obscured by bushes but, whenever it reappeared in view, the figure was there, always beckoning him forward.

Halfway up the hill Leif paused to catch his breath and wipe the beads of sweat from his forehead. He started off again and had just gone a few paces when a voice stopped him.

'Mr Olsen.'

Leif spun round and from behind the bushes emerged Ma Demuth, smiling and clutching her carrier bag tightly against her chest.

32

'Darling, you look pale. Are you all right?'

Juliet nodded but she was still feeling shaky.

'You're sure?' persisted Sir Alec.

'I am, Dad, honest.' Juliet hoped her father would not have noticed, but the shock of seeing the spectral image had shaken her. And she knew she would not get any sympathy from either him or Edward.

'Good,' declared Sir Alec. 'Then we will breakfast.' The old man hesitated and smiled. 'You'll be glad to hear Edward and I are not playing golf today. We'll have a drive round the island. It will do us all good.'

'But—'

'No buts,' cut in Sir Alec. 'We're all going and it will be a nice day out.'

'It will,' agreed Edward. 'And put a bit of colour back in your beautiful face, won't it?'

Juliet ignored this comment and headed out of the suite. The two men followed closely behind, with Edward smiling contentedly.

During breakfast Edward excused himself and phoned Curley. After a few rings, Curley answered in his usual gruff voice.

'It's me,' announced Edward. 'You've received the money?'

'Yeah, but you said—'

'I know what I said,' snapped Edward. 'You'll receive the rest and more. Now listen carefully.' And Edward went through his instructions.

'You can't do that!' Curley exclaimed.

'Can't is not in my vocabulary,' snapped Edward. 'Will you do it or shall I find someone else?'

'It will cost you.'

'I'll double what I've already paid you. Will you do it?'

Curley hesitated. 'It's one hell of a risk, in broad daylight, I mean.'

'That's what you're being paid for. I will phone you just before two.' Edward put the phone down and re-joined Juliet and Sir Alec in the dining room.

'I'd 'oped to see you,' said Ma, advancing towards Leif.

Leif took one look at the aged woman and then back at the gibbet. The beckoning figure was still there, but it was fading fast.

'Can you see 'er?' asked Ma. 'You can, can't you?' Ma edged closer to Leif. 'Mary Hunter. It's 'er what you can see. Or is it 'er at the hotel? They look almost the same, you know.'

The figure on the gibbet had now disappeared and Leif looked back at the old woman. Ma smiled, a sparkle in her stony eyes.

'Who was it? The Hunter girl or your lover?'

'You tell me,' said Leif.

Ma shook her head, all the time staring at him, just as she had done at the Compass.

'They strung 'er up,' she sneered. 'On a cold winter's day, they strung 'er up. For murdering the man she loved. And she's never gone away.'

'You mean Mary Hunter?'

'Who else? She's the only one what 'aunts these parts. Course it's Mary Hunter. And she's been getting stronger.'

'But why?'

Ma continued, ignoring Leif's question. 'I saw you the first day you arrived and I sensed something was 'appening. And that Mary Hunter was coming back. It's 'er legacy, you see.'

'But what does she want?'

Ma gripped the carrier bag even tighter, squashing some of the contents. 'What's she wants? She wants you, she does. And 'er at the hotel. And there's nothing you can do. Not now.'

Just over an hour later Tim Curley perched himself halfway up Gibbet Hill with a packet of crisps and bottle of beer beside him. Around his neck he had a pair of field binoculars, although he did not need them. He could see the campsite quite clearly and was able to watch Mr Robson's attempts to round up his pupils for the day's outing. And he could see Billy Bush and his father bent over the engine of their battered van. And alone in the field below him he watched as Leif Olsen secured the new padlock to his tent before heading out of the campsite.

The clock on St Michael's struck ten and Tim Curley started his bottle of beer.

He watched and waited.

Half an hour later Billy Bush had managed to start the van and the spluttering engine sent clouds of smoke from the exhaust. Rose Bush came to inspect what was going on.

Tim Curley reached for the Swiss Army knife in his pocket and pushed the largest of the blades open. He ran his finger lightly along it, feeling the sharp metal against his skin. It would do the job nicely, he thought.

And as he waited, he started on the packet of crisps. At midday he would make his move.

On leaving the campsite Leif hitched a lift to Narraport in an ex-postal van. The driver dropped him on the outskirts of town, not far from a row of phone boxes. Leif tried the hotel again. A different and younger voice answered it to the previous night.

'This is Mr Olsen,' Leif started. 'Could you put me through to Miss Tyler please.'

'Miss Tyler is not in,' replied Jill.

'Then could you ask her to contact me?' asked Leif. 'She knows where I am.'

'It might not be possible,' replied Jill cautiously, aware that Norman Strevans might be listening in the office.

'Please,' said Leif.

'Goodbye, Mr Olsen,' said Jill firmly, putting the receiver down. Although she did not know the full story, she admired Leif's persistence.

From the phone box, Leif made his way to Narraport library, a large imposing building built, according to the plaque, in 1889. The library was well stocked but on a hot day was empty, apart from three librarians bickering over work rotas.

He noticed a sign pointing to the reference library and he ran up the stairs, two at a time. An elderly spectacled man at the enquiry desk looked at Leif as he approached. It was the first enquirer he'd had that day.

'I'm interested in local history,' Leif began. 'Old criminal cases and cases of hauntings.'

The man adjusted his half-moon spectacles, eased himself up and held out his hand.

'I am Archibald McGee, Secretary of the local history society. I am also president of the SGC.'

'SGC?' queried Leif.

'Scurra Ghost Club,' the man replied. 'How can I help?'

It was not until early afternoon when Paul Chase remembered the paper he had been carrying in his wallet. He pulled it out and re-read what Leif had written. If he left it in Juliet Tyler's room it was then up to her whether she contacted him or not – at least he would have honoured his promise.

Paul ran up the stairs from the kitchen to the ground floor. He had hoped it was a good opportunity to see Jill and get the keys to the Dickens Suite. But Jill was being harangued by Katherine Strevans. Jill glanced in his direction and looked despairingly to the ceiling, exasperated at the additional directives she was being giving.

Paul kept close to the wall and stealthily made his way up to the first and then second floor.

Cherie was vacuuming, her back turned away from him.

'Cherie.'

The French girl did not hear.

Paul reached over and tapped her shoulder. Cherie jumped and jerked back. 'You scare me!' she exclaimed with a relieved laugh.

'Sorry, love. Look, Cherie, have you got the keys to the Dickens Suite?'

The cleaner shook her head. 'No, only Jill 'as.'

'Or me.' Ann Walker came out of room 28 and looked at the chef enquiringly. 'Why do you want them, Paul?'

'To deliver a message to Miss Tyler.'

'Really?' Ann raised her eyebrows. 'Whatever would Jill say?'

'No, it's not from me,' protested Paul. 'Someone has asked me to give it to her.'

Ann looked dubiously at Paul. It was not that she disbelieved him but wondered how such an important guest would react to a message being left in her room, or indeed what Norman or Katherine Strevans would say if they found out.

'Mademoiselle Tyler 'as an admirer?' asked Cherie.

Paul nodded. 'And I promised to give the message to her,' he added.

'What sort of message is it?'

'It's written on a scrap of paper. It won't take a moment to put in her room.'

'Very well, then,' said Ann and she reached in her pocket and handed Paul a set of master keys. 'It's this one,' she said indicating a silver Yale key. 'Perhaps you'd like to go in with Paul,' she added looking over at Cherie.

Paul took the keys and the two made their way along the corridor to the Dickens Suite.

'I take it they're out?' asked Paul.

'I think so,' replied Cherie. 'But we 'ad better check.' She knocked at the door and they waited. When there was no reply, Paul turned the key and the two entered.

'It's over here,' said Cherie, indicating the furthest door.

Paul followed Cherie over to Juliet's door. Again, they knocked and waited.

'It might not be locked,' whispered Cherie.

Paul tried the door, but it didn't open. He unlocked it and entered. The sun shone brightly through the window and the room smelt clean and fresh. 'It's a bit cold,' he commented.

Cherie considered Paul's remark and nodded. *'Oui,'* she agreed. 'It is. It is always a strange room.'

'And it's such a hot day.'

Puzzled, Paul went over to the window and despite the warm rays that filtered through the glass and the heat outside, the room felt distinctly chilly.

'Is it usually this cold?' he asked.

Cherie shrugged her shoulders. 'It is Ann who usually cleans it,' she replied. She turned. 'It sound as if she comes. We'll ask her.'

The two waited and when no one appeared Paul went over to Juliet's door and looked into the suite.

'Strange. I'm sure I heard someone.'

'Oui,' said Cherie, joining Paul. 'So did I. But there is no one there.'

The drive round Scurra was at a leisurely pace. Edward drove with Juliet, at Sir Alec's insistence, sitting with him at the front.

They stopped at a converted windmill for a mid-morning drink and at a thatched pub for what proved a disappointing lunch.

By early afternoon they had reached Pear Beach and, at Sir Alec's suggestion, Edward parked the car to get some ice creams.

Pear Beach was busy. Almost all the deckchairs were occupied and the holiday crowd lay stretched out on the sand, some asleep, some reading, some listening to music. Juliet noticed several families, the parents instructing their children on the fine art of sandcastle building and there was one child, about eight, with a mass of ginger hair, burying his father in the sand. Juliet thought of Leif and of what Pear Beach had meant to him.

'This is awful,' declared Edward. 'We'd have been better going somewhere quieter.'

Sir Alec smiled. 'Pear Beach is famous,' he replied. 'You can't come to Scurra without seeing Pear Beach.'

'I could,' retorted Edward. 'Easily.'

Sir Alec stopped and looked beyond the sunbathers to the wide stretches of sand and to the many swimming and splashing in the calm waters. 'You can see why it's so popular. It's ideal for young families.' Sir Alec glanced at Juliet, still watching the ginger haired boy squealing with delight as he heaped more sand over his father.

'Is anything wrong?' he asked, seeing Juliet so preoccupied.

'Yes,' she said. 'I want to go back to the hotel.'

Frantically Alan Bridgeway ran up the path to the Bush Retreat and pressed on the doorbell. Moments later Rose Bush opened the door and stared at the flustered boy.

'Whatever is the matter?' she asked.

'It's the tent,' panted Alan. 'In the far field.'

'What about it?'

'Someone's attacking it with a knife.'

'Never!' exclaimed Rose in disbelief.

'Honest, Mrs Bush,' insisted the boy.

'Then I'd better take a look,' said Rose uneasily. 'Thomas,' she called. 'Billy. Come quick. An emergency.'

And she waited for her two menfolk to join her before all three tore across the campsite to see what was happening.

33

Turner and Williams sat in their patrol car just off the main road that ran through Lower Arch. It was a shadowy spot and ideal for trapping speeding motorists. Most of the holiday makers were no problem. Unfamiliar with the twists and turns of the roads they tended to drive slowly and with care. However, the residents, familiar with the roads, took more chances and were ideal prey.

Turner, hot and weary, lay back in the driver's seat and closed his eyes.

'Let me know if you see something,' he yawned.

Williams nodded.

'On one condition,' he said.

'What?'

'You buy me an ice cream later.'

'Done.'

Several cars passed, all within the speed limit, all the drivers unaware of the hidden police car. There was a lull in the traffic and then a Peugeot Estate flashed by. Williams glanced over at his dozing colleague.

'Fancy some action?'

'Not yet.'

Williams continued to watch.

'Hey!' he exclaimed, giving his colleague a nudge. 'Look over there.'

Turner roused himself and saw who Williams was pointing to. Tim Curley was making his way down Lower Arch High Street. He was walking quickly and purposefully.

'Are you thinking what I am thinking?' Williams asked.

'Hotel thefts?'

Williams nodded. 'Could be. But he's been up to something. That's for sure.'

Turner started the car and headed towards Curley.

After a chocolate chip ice cream from Betty's Famous Ice Cream Parlour, Edward began the leisurely drive back to the hotel. He drove slowly and several times glanced at Juliet's shapely legs through her cotton dress. Juliet seemed unaware of his glances.

They arrived back at the hotel at four. Edward and Sir Alec went straight to the bar in search of refreshment while Juliet returned to the suite.

As soon as she entered her room she saw the folded receipt propped against the vase. Intrigued, she opened it, recognising the writing immediately. It read:

Dear Juliet,
Desperately trying to contact. I love you, <u>please</u> come and see me
Leif xxx

Juliet re-read the note and smiled. She didn't know how Leif had managed to get the message into her room, but it was all she had hoped. She just had time to slip out and see him before dinner.

As the police car approached Curley from behind, Williams wound down his window.

'Good afternoon, Tim.'

Curley shot a startled look at the car and, recognising who it was, broke into a frantic and ungainly run.

Williams smiled. 'Maybe it won't be such a quiet afternoon after all,' he mused.

Turner accelerated the car and followed Curley to the alley where Williams took up the pursuit on foot. He knew the overweight and already breathless Curley could not carry on for too long and that quite soon, given Curley's past performances, they were in for an entertaining time at the Station.

As Juliet swung the Rolls down the unmade road she noticed a police car heading towards her. She stopped and reversed onto the grass curb to let the car pass. When it was clear Juliet continued up the road, puzzled at the appearance of officialdom. She pulled up outside the Bush Retreat and immediately a flustered Rose Bush rushed out of the house.

'Oh, my dear!' she gasped. 'What an afternoon.'

'What's the matter?' asked Juliet, alarmed.

'It's Leif. His tent's been slashed.'

'Slashed!' exclaimed Juliet in disbelief.

Rose nodded vigorously, sending ripples down her ample neck.

'It was lucky one of Mr Robson's lads spotted Curley before he did too much damage and we chased him off. I reported it straight to the police. And the day before Curley broke into Leif's tent. A proper rotten egg, he is.'

'And where's Leif?' asked Juliet.

Rose looked at her. 'I think you'd better come indoors, love,' she said. 'There's something I need to tell you.'

Juliet followed Rose into the house. Inside was a clutter and Juliet had to pick her way through the various boots and shoes discarded in the hallway. The living room was no better and Rose hurriedly retrieved a pile of newspapers and music magazines from one of the chairs so Juliet could sit down. Rose drew up a chair opposite.

'As I was saying,' she continued. 'It was Curley what did it. And a good job he was spotted too. There's no telling what he would have done. Anyway, we put the police on him straight away.'

'I just saw the police leave,' said Juliet. 'But where's

Leif? Has he been hurt or something?'

Rose shook her head. 'Oh no.' She hesitated. 'But he did seem in a bit of a daze. As if something was troubling him. Not just his tent, I mean, and he was pretty angry about that, I can tell you.' Rose stopped and regarded Juliet thoughtfully. 'Look dear, I feel dreadful. I told Leif a lie.'

Juliet looked enquiringly at Rose.

'There's this woman, Ma Demuth,' said Rose. 'She's a strange old bird. Has visions and all that sort of thing. Well she came 'ere one day issuing warnings. She said something was going to happen to Leif, and particularly if he takes up with you.'

'With me?'

'That's right. Well, Leif was walking past the other day and he says to me that he saw Ma Demuth in 'ere. He took me all by surprise when he said it. It quite threw me, especially with all the warnings Ma had been going on about. So, I said she wasn't 'ere, but she was.' Rose shook her head. 'I don't often lie, but I was all of a dither. I mean, Ma is such a strange one and I didn't know what to tell him.' Rose leaned forward, her rickety chair moving with her weight. 'Look, love,' she said. 'has anything been happening at your hotel?'

'How do you mean?'

'Strange things,' said Rose. 'It has, hasn't it?'

'Yes,' admitted Juliet. 'Things have been happening. But where is Leif?'

'What sort of things?' persisted Rose.

Juliet moved uncomfortably. 'My room is haunted.'

'Haunted?'

Juliet nodded. 'By a young woman called Mary Hunter.'

'And . . .and 'ave you seen this Mary Hunter?'

'I did this morning. I saw a faint image of a young woman.'

'Oh, my poor love,' sympathised Rose. 'Ma was right, you know, something strange is going on.'

'Yes, but you still haven't told me where Leif is.'

'He's with Ann Walker.' Rose paused. 'You see, Leif came back this afternoon and apparently he'd found something out about this Hunter girl. I told him about his tent and, well when he calmed down, he said he had to see you. That it was vital. He spoke to the police and dashed off, much to their annoyance.'

'And who's Ann Walker?'

'She's a cleaner at the hotel. Been there for years, she has. I went to school with her, that's how I know her.'

'But why's he seeing her?'

'Because he says he's got to see you.'

'So why can't he go straight to the hotel?'

'The Strevans' won't let him in. He tried last night and Norman Strevans and your dad's friend threw him out. Got quite violent, they did. I told him that if anyone knew how to get into the hotel it would be Ann. That's why he went.'

'Where does Ann live?'

'The Cottage, Lower Arch. It's a small white thatched cottage, just off the high street. Real pretty it is. You can't miss it.'

'How long ago did he leave?'

Rose shrugged her shoulders. 'Maybe forty minutes ago. He'd be there by now.'

Juliet eased herself up from her chair. 'I'll try and track him down.'

Rose nodded. 'Well, do be careful, love. I'm real worried. Worried for you both.' Rose hesitated. 'You see, if Mary Hunter is still around, goodness knows what could happen. She killed her lover, she did, and was hung.' Rose stood up, looked at Juliet a moment before reaching over and giving her a hug. 'Please be careful, love. I'd hate anything bad to happen.'

34

As Leif approached Lower Arch he stopped by a roadside stream and sloshed some water over his face. He was hot, sticky and his feet slightly swollen. He had already walked over twelve miles, a lot of it in the heat of the day, and apart from an orange, a choc ice and some biscuits Rose had given him, he'd had little refreshment.

He was angry about his tent. Curley had damaged it beyond use leaving him no option but to sleep rough or go home. He had no doubt that Edward Harrison was behind the attack, but Harrison was too clever to have any blame attached to him. It was unlikely Curley had ever seen Harrison or even knew his name.

He thought too of how he could get into the hotel and see Juliet. It was more important than ever that he contacted her, especially after what the historian, Archibald McGee, had told him.

Leif found Ann Walker's cottage set a little way off the main road and not far from the centre of Lower Arch. With its freshly thatched roof and abundant garden, it was so typically English. Rambling roses zigzagged their way up the newly painted stone walls and the delphiniums and hollyhocks were as resplendent as any Leif had seen.

He quickly ran a comb through his damp hair and pressed the doorbell. Moments later Ann appeared with a little dog yapping at her feet. She was much as he had imagined her – the same age as Rose Bush, although slimmer and far better groomed.

'Mr Olsen,' she said, holding the door open. 'Rose said you'd be coming over. You look hot. Do come in. This is Dizzy.'

Leif entered the well-appointed cottage.

'Like a tea?'

'I'd love one,' replied Leif as he entered a cosy lounge.

'Do take a seat.'

Leif settled in one of the comfy chairs, gazing a moment at the collection of pottery animals arranged above the inglenook fireplace. Two racks of thimbles hung on either side of an embroidery, probably one Ann had done herself. He heard her switch the kettle on before she came back to join him. Dizzy stayed closely by her side.

'I'm not sure I can help you, you know,' she began.

Leif looked up at her. 'I must get into the hotel,' he said. 'Juliet Tyler is in danger.'

Ann Walker pursed her lips thoughtfully. 'What makes you think that?'

'Because of things that are happening. Juliet has been disturbed at night. There have been noises, been—'

'I know,' interrupted Ann. 'I've heard about them.'

'And it's connected with Mary Hunter.' Leif paused. 'I don't know if you know about it, but Mary Hunter committed a murder in the room where Juliet is staying. Juliet swears that her ghost has now returned. Miss Walker, I have got to get into the hotel.'

Ann Walker looked a moment at Leif. 'Mr Olsen,' she began slowly. 'Are you familiar with Ma Demuth?'

'I am.'

'Well, she is a very odd person to say the least. But one night, last Monday it was, she stopped me in most curious circumstances and asked if anything had happened to 'er upstairs. At the time I didn't understand but I now realise she was referring to Juliet Tyler.'

'Did she say anything else?'

Ann shook her head. 'No, but she said enough. And there have been other things. Archie Cann, the odd job man, told me a friend of his had found something odd in that room once, and another cleaner, Cherie, thought she saw someone standing behind me when I was cleaning the room. So, Mr Olsen, I do believe you when you say there is something strange going on.' Ann paused. 'But what exactly do you want me to do?'

'I want you to get me into the hotel.'

'Why don't you see Mr and Mrs Strevans?'

'Because they won't let me in. Last night Strevans and Harrison threw me out.' Leif hesitated. 'Harrison is doing all he can to stop me from seeing Juliet. She mentioned that he'd been pestering her a lot of late. I think he wants her for himself. But she doesn't love him, Ann, I know she doesn't!'

Ann looked at him sympathetically. It was obvious that Leif was certainly in love with Juliet.

'Rose told me about your tent. You think he was responsible?'

'Positive. He wants me off the island. He even said I'd lose the job I've been promised if I did not leave. And he has the influence and contacts to make it happen.'

'And Juliet is worth more than the job?' enquired Ann raising her eyebrows.

'She's worth more than anything,' replied Leif. 'Ann, I've got to protect her and I've got to get into that hotel.'

Ann looked thoughtfully at Leif for a moment and then returned to the kitchen to make the tea. Dizzy followed.

When she returned, she carried two steaming mugs of tea on a tray and two chunks of fruit cake.

'If I get you into the hotel,' she said slowly. 'What do you intend to do?'

'I must to talk to Juliet. There are things I've found out.'

'And what if Mr Harrison sees you, or Norman or Katherine Strevans? They will wonder how you got into the hotel and that will put me in a rather invidious position.'

'Miss Walker,' said Leif solemnly. 'I assure you, if anything goes wrong I will not mention your name. I promise. I'll take any flak on myself.'

Ann Walker reached over to the tray and put a slice of cake on a side plate and passed it to Leif.

'I will help you,' she said slowly. 'I will help you because Rose has asked me to help you. And because I *do* believe there is a serious problem in Miss Tyler's room. But . . .' Ann was interrupted by a knocking at the front door. 'Excuse me,' she started. 'This could be my friend Elsie.'

Ann Walker got to her feet and went through to the hallway. Leif heard the door opening and then a familiar voice asking if he was there.

As soon as he recognised Juliet's voice, Leif leapt to his feet and raced through to the hallway. Juliet and Leif looked at each other a moment before Leif reached forward and embraced her, kissing the side of her head.

'Excuse me,' said Ann, concerned any passers-by had noticed what was going on. 'I think you had better come in.'

Leif let Juliet in, noticing her eyes were bloodshot and moist.

'It's going to be all right, darling,' he whispered.

Juliet clasped her hands together, her eyes full of fear. She followed Leif through to the lounge.

Ann closed the door behind them. 'I'll make another tea,' she said, and thankfully withdrew to the kitchen.

'You got my note?'

Juliet nodded and watched as Leif pulled a badly creased handkerchief out of his pocket. He wiped away a tear that was running down her cheek.

'They told me some dreadful things,' whispered Juliet.

'About me?'

Juliet nodded.

'Like what?'

'That you'd got a record.'

'A what!'

'You'd been in trouble with the police. And—'

'But that's nonsense,' snapped Leif. 'Who said that?'

'My father.'

'What else?'

'That you'd lived with someone for three years. Barbara somebody.'

'Barbara Anstey,' said Leif. He shook his head and turned to face her. 'Darling, you mustn't believe them.'

'But they said . . .'

'They've distorted the truth. Barbara Anstey and I shared a house in Bournemouth for three years. She was a flatmate and no more. She was on the same course as me and,' added Leif with a smile, 'got married the moment the course ended. Honestly Juliet, they've distorted things.'

'But what about the police?'

'That was stupid.' Leif sighed. 'It was something crazy I did. But it's nothing to worry about.'

Juliet swallowed and waited.

'Okay. The thing with the police. After the first-year exams I went out on a binge and it got out of hand.'

'And?'

'I got done ... well, several of us got done ... for being drunk and disorderly. But Juliet, that was all. How your father found out, I don't know. Not even my mum knows.' Leif paused. 'I've nothing to hide. And I love you.'

Ann Walker appeared carrying a third mug of tea and a portion of cake.

'And I'll have you know,' said Ann to Juliet, 'that not only has Mr Olsen's tent been wrecked but he's probably lost his job.'

'Never!'

'You tell her,' said Ann looking across at Leif.

Leif shook his head.

'It's . . .'

'You must tell me,' urged Juliet. 'What about your job?'

Leif sighed. 'Harrison said if I didn't get off Scurra this morning I'd lose my job at Sibley's.'

'But he can't do that!' protested Juliet.

'He's got influence. Anyway, that's not important. What I need to do is get into the hotel.'

'Is there any point?' asked Ann. 'You've seen Miss Tyler now.'

'I have to.'

'Why?' asked Juliet.

'Because I have to meet Mary Hunter.'

'What!'

'No arguing,' interrupted Leif. 'I have to stay in your room tonight, Juliet. I have to.'

Juliet gaped at him. 'But what about Dad? Edward? It's not possible. That damned Edward has a habit of just walking into my room.'

'Does he indeed,' said Leif grimly. 'If he walks in on me, I'll brain him with something. We'll make sure the door's locked.'

'I'm scared Leif!'

'Juliet,' said Leif firmly. 'We're almost at the end now. You must have faith in me. I know what I'm doing.'

'I can arrange it,' said Ann slowly. 'Maybe you, Miss Tyler, can stay in Jill's room. Jill usually spends the night in her boyfriend Paul's room,' she explained. 'She's not supposed to, of course.'

'That sounds ideal,' said Leif with some satisfaction. 'Tonight, I will at last be able to meet this wretched ghost.'

35

Juliet returned to the hotel just before six while Leif remained at the cottage. Ann prepared a cheese salad for them both and while they ate she explained how he could get into the hotel unnoticed.

At half past seven Leif announced it was time for him to go.

'Not yet,' said Ann in surprise. 'It's too light.'

'I won't be heading straight to the hotel,' replied Leif. 'There is someone I need to see. Someone who holds the key to the whole mystery.

'Ma Demuth?'

Leif smiled. 'No. The owner of Scurra General Stores.'

'What, scruffy old Steve what's-his-name?'

'Yes,' said Leif. 'Him.'

Edward dialled the local number – the second time that afternoon. The first time there was no reply, the second a woman answered. Edward hung up immediately, wondering where Tim Curley was.

After dinner Sir Alec, Edward and Juliet returned to the suite, and Sir Alec took out an old carved chess set from the sideboard.

'I propose a tournament,' he declared. 'You and Edward against me. It's a challenge.'

'But Dad,' protested Juliet. 'You know I'm no good at chess.'

'Never let me hear you say that,' said Sir Alec. 'You must never talk yourself down. Besides, I am sure Edward will help.'

Sir Alec handed Edward the box of pieces to set up while he went to the drinks cabinet to pour himself, Juliet and Edward a gin and tonic.

Edward glanced over at Juliet and winked. 'Might as well keep your father happy,' he said and began to place the pieces on the board. Sir Alec re-joined them, put the drinks down and helped put the final pieces into position.

'Right,' he declared. 'Let battle commence.'

Juliet opened by moving a pawn.

Sir Alec's eyes sparkled. For once he had a good colour and his mind was sharp and incisive. So different from the occasional lethargic manner that had afflicted him since his coronary. He played his move swiftly and Edward responded. Edward's concentration was absolute and he was determined not to let the old man beat him. There was pride at stake.

Juliet watched the moves. Her father lost a pawn and rook, but quickly retaliated. It was going to be a long battle.

She eased herself up from the settee and went through to her own room. Despite the heat of the day it felt chill. And Juliet knew she was not alone. Lurking somewhere, unseen, was Mary Hunter. She feared for Leif. He had said it was vital to spend the night in her room and despite her pleading and the risks, nothing would dissuade him.

Juliet slipped on a cardigan and went through to the main room. Her father was staring intently at the board. Edward looked up.

'Going out?' he enquired.

'Just downstairs,' replied Juliet. And she left the suite and went to the reception to speak to Jill.

Leif went around to the side of the Scurra General Stores and knocked at the shabby white door. He could hear the noise of the television, turned almost to full volume. He waited and knocked again. This time he was heard.

There was a jangle of keys, the door opened and the

old shopkeeper peered out. 'What d'you want?' he snapped. He smelt of drink.

'I need to speak to you. It's very important.'

'Well, you can't. I'm watching telly.' The shopkeeper started to close the door, but Leif jammed his foot in the way.

'It concerns Mary Hunter.'

'Who?' asked the old man, his eyes narrowing.

'Mary Hunter,' repeated Leif. 'The young woman who was hung for murdering her lover.'

'What's that to do with me?'

'A lot,' said Leif. 'Now can I come in?'

The old man regarded him warily and then reluctantly opened the door and let him in.

At quarter to ten, Juliet returned to the Dickens Suite. Edward and her father were still locked in combat. Both had lost more pieces and the game was delicately poised.

'Good game?' she enquired.

'Shh!' snapped Edward.

Her father winked at her. Victory was not far off.

'Good night.' She bent and kissed the top of her father's head and he smiled up at her.

She then went through to her room, locking the door behind her. The room was not as cold as before and she sensed Mary Hunter had, for the moment, gone.

Juliet drew the curtains, took the Steelgate book from off her dressing table and stretched out on her bed. Idly she began to flick through the pages. It was going to be a long night. One she would never forget.

36

'Juliet.'

Juliet saw her door knob turn.

'Juliet.'

It was Edward. She knew he would come and that if she let him in he would rape her. Ever since he thought he had disposed of Leif he had become bolder. He wanted to own her. Maybe her father had goaded him on, telling him what a good wife she would make. But for once Sir Alec was wrong. She would never let Edward near her again. Not after the lies he had told about Leif.

'Juliet. It's me,' whispered Edward urgently. 'I must see you.'

He tried the door again, but Juliet lay still on the bed. She hoped he would think her asleep and eventually go.

'Juliet,' Edward said once more, this time rattling the door. Still Juliet did not move.

At last she heard him return to his room. It was 10:55. Leif would be in the hotel grounds by now and she wondered what he had found out.

From behind a shrub Leif surveyed the hotel. He could see Norman Strevans talking to a guest in the lobby and bidding him good night. The lights in the hotel were gradually turned off as the guests retired for the night.

It was at 2.30 in the morning when the murder was committed. Despite the intervening years, and the modernisation that had taken place, Mary Hunter would still be able to recognise much of the building. Maybe, on that fateful night, she had passed through the grounds where Leif was now. And yet at the time murder was possibly the last thing on her mind. But the moment she entered her room, events had taken their tragic course and from then on, Mary

Hunter had not been able to rest in peace.
Tonight, he would confront Mary Hunter.

Juliet continued to study the Steelgate collection. Often, she paused, examining the fine details of some of the artist's work. As she was admiring the painting of Scurra rock, she noticed her curtains start to ripple. And the temperature once again began to fall.
She swung herself off the bed and unlocked the door.
It was 10 to midnight.

Edward Harrison could not sleep. The chess game had stimulated him. After the twentieth move he had fought for a draw, but still Sir Alec played on; relentlessly, craftily. And finally, he'd been outmanoeuvred and trapped.
He did not like losing; it made him annoyed with himself.
His mind wandered from chess to Juliet. He had hoped to have her tonight, to make passionate love to her; the more she resisted, the more frantic grew his longing to possess her. Obviously, her little crush on Olsen, interesting to her probably because he was so different to the men she usually dated, had prevented him from breaching her reserve. Now that he had shown Olsen up for the fraudster he was, there was no competition. He had taken the precaution of slipping a pill into Sir Alec's last gin and tonic and could hear the old man's snores from here. By his bed, across the chair, lay a long grey silk scarf. He hated to do it but if Juliet showed signs of screaming, he would just have to gag her. He was convinced she'd enjoy the struggle. Women always pretended they hated it, but in the end, he had found they wanted his lovemaking so much he had a job getting rid of them when he was tired of them.
Would he ever tire of Juliet? He might. But

nonetheless, he would make sure he married her and was in charge of her money.

He looked over to the clock on his bedside cabinet and it was then that he heard a slight movement in her room.

He lay still and listened.

Leif skirted round the back of the hotel and identified the green door that Ann Walker had mentioned. She had warned him of the security light at the back and which would come on the moment he crossed its beam. She hoped no one would notice. Often a fox or cat set it off.

Leif reached for the key Ann had given him. Usually the door would have been bolted from the inside, but Ann had spoken to Jill and arranged that it would remain unbolted. It was a risk both were taking, but Ann had impressed on Jill the gravity of the situation.

Swiftly, silently, Leif emerged from the shadows and darted across the path to the green door. The security light clicked on, casting a strong beam. He inserted the key, unlocked the door and entered. The kitchen was large, clean and smelt of disinfectant.

He locked the door behind him and crossed the damp floor. Ann had warned him it might be slippery. It was always washed last thing at night. He reached the furthest door and opened it. This was the door Ann had mentioned might be noisy and, as he pressed against it, the door let out an ominous squeak. He passed through, held the door still a moment and then let it swing shut, letting out another squeak as it did so.

He thought he heard a voice from upstairs. Several voices. Then all went quiet.

Gingerly, Leif climbed the stairs in front of him. These were the stairs the servants would have used and avoided the hotel lobby and front of the building.

At the top, he again waited, listened and watched.

Across the corridor was a stairway.

A door opened.

Leif froze.

Footsteps.

Silence.

Leif darted across the corridor and swiftly up three more flights coming to the landing Ann had described to him. He saw the first door she had mentioned marked PRIVATE. This was one of the linen cupboards. The next door was Cherie's, then Jill's.

Silently, apprehensively, Leif made his way down the corridor to the third door.

He turned the handle and entered. The room was in darkness.

'Leif, is that you?'

'Juliet.'

Leif swiftly closed the door and turned on the light. A worried-looking Juliet, still wearing her daytime clothes, was waiting for him.

'You made it,' she declared with a sigh of relief.

Leif took her in his arms and kissed her.

'How are you?' he whispered.

'Nervous,' she replied. She studied Leif's earnest features. 'Look, I think Mary Hunter is in my room. The temperature began to fall and the curtains started to move. I couldn't see her but I'm positive she's there. Oh, Leif, why don't we spend the night in this room. It will be safe until morning.'

He shook his head. 'No,' he said firmly. 'I must go to your room. I have . . .'

'But why?' interrupted Juliet. 'It's . . .'

'Shh.' Leif put a finger to Juliet's lips. 'Darling, don't argue. I'm going.'

'But she's a murderess. She was hung. And I'm sure she's there. Please don't go, please.'

'She's dead, she can't murder anyone now. Look, I'm going,' Leif insisted. 'Stay here until I'm back. Okay?'

Juliet nodded. 'Please be careful.'

'I will.' And with a final kiss, Leif returned to the dark corridor, headed towards the front of the hotel and down the one flight of stairs that brought him to the Dickens Suite.

Edward switched on his bedside light and eased himself out of bed. Making hardly any noise he opened his own door and looked around the darkened room. All was still, just as he and Sir Alec had left it before they had retired. Sir Alec had ceased snoring quite so loudly, but his breathing was heavy. He was sound asleep, no need to worry about him. Edward crept over to Juliet's door and listened. Silence. He reached for the door knob and tried it. To his pleasant surprise, he found the door unlocked. Clutching the scarf in his hand, he advanced into the room and saw, in the half light, that the bed was empty and that Juliet was not there.

The room felt cold. Unwelcoming.

Puzzled, he crept back to his own room, gently closing his door after him. Where could she have possibly gone? The bed had looked unused. A midnight stroll? Surely not. He lay on his bed and waited.

Silently, Leif unlocked the door with the key Ann had given him and entered the suite. He was surprised at the size of the main room and even in the half light, could discern the sheer splendour of the furnishings.

He quickly identified the three bedroom doors and could hear rumbling snores coming from Sir Alec's room. The next door along was Edward Harrison's and the furthest door Juliet's.

Slowly he advanced towards it, the sound of his movement being cushioned by the thick pile carpet.

He opened Juliet's door and entered, closing the door silently after him.

The room was cool. Unnaturally so. But it was all still, all quiet.

As his eyes adjusted to the dim light, Leif saw a large book on Juliet's dressing table. It was the Steelgate Collection, the book Juliet had mentioned to him. Beside the book was a new vase of sweet peas, giving a pleasant fragrance to the room.

Leif went across to the curtains. They were still now, but like Juliet, he was certain it was the ghost of Mary Hunter who had moved them.

He parted the curtains a little and looked out. It was a bright, calm night, the moon casting shadows over the countryside with the few clouds there were illuminated like cotton puffs. Looming in the background was the unmistakable rise of Gibbet Hill, the hill where Mary Hunter's body had been taken after the hanging.

Leif heard a creak behind him and swung round. He could see no one but he knew he was not alone.

'Mary,' he whispered. 'Is that you?'

Another creak. Silence. The temperature of the room began to drop even further and Leif wondered how Juliet had managed to stay in the room for so long. Maybe it was fear of her father or of Edward, neither of whom believed her. Or because the Strevans had insisted everything was all right. He wondered how much those two knew. The ghost of Mary Hunter had been seen before, even though her appearance was irregular and then only on certain occasions. It was all part of her tragic legacy.

The pipe under the floorboard gurgled and the numbers on the clock changed to 12:29.

Leif stretched out on the bed and thought of Juliet, safe in one of the rooms above him. He wondered if she was asleep yet. If she could rest more easily now that she was in a different room.

There was another gurgle, then the sound of movement outside Juliet's door. And the door knob began to turn.

Jill made sure Paul was asleep before she slipped out of bed and back along the corridor to her own bedroom. She wore only a skimpy nightie – one that Paul had bought her as a present.

She opened the door of her room and entered.

'Who is it?' Juliet demanded, sitting upright in bed.

'It's only me,' said Jill. 'I couldn't sleep. I didn't mean to disturb you. I just wanted to make sure everything was all right.'

'As right as it can be.'

'Did Leif get into the hotel?'

'Yes. Oh, Jill, he's gone to the suite. I begged him not to go but he said he must.' Juliet paused. 'He's found something out about her ... Mary Hunter.'

The moment Leif saw the door knob move, he sprang off the bed and darted to the far side of the room, squeezing himself between the wall and wardrobe.

Edward entered the room, his eyes wandering from the now crumpled and empty bed to the half-drawn curtains. He frowned. What game was she playing with him now? Was this all part of her idea of foreplay? Teasing him into this state of intense longing and pain?

Leif held his breath, pressing himself further into the recess.

'Juliet, is that you?' Edward asked. There was no response. He waited a moment and then leant over the bed and felt the warmth of the duvet.

'Juliet,' he said again. 'Stop hiding from me, stop playing. Come here to me!' Slowly, cautiously he advanced into the room.

The pipe under the floor gurgled.

'Juliet?'

Edward drew level with Leif, his eyes fixed upon the window. Then, in an instance, he spun round and faced Leif.

'You!' he spat. 'You!'

He lunged at Leif and Leif, pressing his foot against the wall, propelled himself forward, pushing Edward to the ground, falling on top of him and desperately trying to pin his shoulders to the ground. But Edward was taller, stronger, bigger. He jerked himself up, sending Leif sprawling.

'You bastard!' seethed Edward. 'You're going to pay for this.'

Leif struggled to his feet and Edward once more lunged at him, sending him to the floor. Leif kicked back, catching Edward and sending him sprawling on the bed. Leif struggled to his feet and Edward reached out, grabbing Leif's shirt and ripping off several buttons as he did so.

Leif took a swipe at Edward, connecting with his chin. Edward yelped and with a sudden jerk of his leg, tripped Leif up and sent him crashing to the floor.

For a second Edward stood above Leif, a wild fury in his eyes.

Leif tried to rise but Edward put his foot on his chest, pinning him to the ground. It was then that Leif noticed the door starting to open and from where he lay he could see a female entering the room. The face was obscured by long flowing black hair and the woman wore a brown tunic.

'Mary!' cried Leif.

Edward turned and gasped as he saw the presence in the doorway.

Slowly the figure moved forward and Edward watched, mesmerised. Leif pushed Edward's foot away and scrambled to his feet. And he watched the strange figure turn to face his adversary and, with long, blood-stained fingers, reach up and push her hair away from her face.

Whatever Edward saw made him freeze in his tracks and a strange gurgling came from his throat as if he was having a stroke. He tried to speak but no words came.

The woman, her back to Leif, moved closer to Edward and with a choking sound, Edward collapsed on the floor.

'What the hell is going on?'

The noise of their fight had penetrated even Sir Alec's deep sleep. He now stood, swaying slightly in the doorway, taking in the incredible scene. The ghostly figure, her features once more obscured by her long black hair, moved towards the window.

'What the . . .' Sir Alec broke off as he and Leif watched the tragic figure of Mary Hunter fade into nothingness.

37

Sir Alec, Juliet and Leif watched from Sir Alec's window as the ambulance pulled away taking Edward Harrison, still deep in shock, to hospital. Below the window, they could see an agitated Katherine Strevans talking in frantic whispers to her husband.

When the ambulance was no longer in view, Sir Alec drew the curtains and went through to the suite. Leif and Juliet followed. Saying nothing and wrapping his silk dressing gown around him, Sir Alec sat in the seat he had used for the chess match. Leif and Juliet placed themselves opposite him on the settee.

Sir Alec looked pale. 'So,' he said at last. 'Perhaps you could explain yourself, Mr Olsen.'

Leif moved uneasily. With his torn shirt, bruised left eye and stubble on his face, he felt unkempt. And yet this was the man he so wanted to impress.

'Sir Alec,' he began slowly. 'To explain what happened tonight, I need to tell you about the ghost you and I saw, the ghost of Mary Hunter. Mary Hunter lived here with her parents in this building in the early part of the nineteenth century.'

'Did I really see her?' queried Sir Alec almost fretfully, 'I was half asleep. Maybe I was dreaming.'

'We both saw her. You know we did.'

Juliet stirred. 'Excuse me,' she said and getting up, went to her room.

Leif went on, regardless of the old man's doubtful expression. 'Mary Hunter was young and pretty and very much like Juliet in looks. Long black hair and . . .'

'Here she is,' interrupted Juliet, returning with the Steelgate book open in her hands. She pointed to Mary Hunter standing by her meek mother. Sir Alec glanced at the painting and then back at Leif. 'There *is* a vague resemblance,' he said grudgingly, 'but so what?'

'From all accounts Mary Hunter was a lively girl and popular with the locals. And she befriended a local lad called John Games and fell very much in love with him.' Leif paused. 'Now Mary's father, John Hunter, was a gambler and had fallen on bad times. One day a distinguished young man called Andrew Squires came to stay in the lodge. He was rich, had a fine reputation and a glittering career in front of him. In later years he became Lord Tetherington and was one of the most successful engineers of his time. He was also a friend of Dickens,' added Leif.

Sir Alec nodded. 'I have heard of him.'

'Well, Squires was good-looking, intelligent, a marvellous raconteur and he had money. And Mary Hunter fell, as did so many, under his spell.

'Her father, with his financial problems, saw Squires as a saviour and exerted enormous pressure on Mary to marry him. The local lad, Games, had no chance against a wealthy and educated suitor. All he had was his love and respect for Mary, and he did not want to lose her.

'On one of Squires' visits to the lodge, John Games decided to confront Squires, the man who had stolen his girl. One night, he crept into Squires' room – the room that is now Juliet's room – and faced Squires. They argued and fought. Games had a knife and, in the struggle, Squires was injured and . . .' Leif broke off and looked over at Juliet. 'Do you remember that picture in the Winderley book which showed Squires with a scar on his face? He got that in the struggle with Games.

'Anyhow,' Leif continued. 'Mary Hunter, hearing the struggle, came into the room, saw the knife which Games had probably dropped, picked it up and tried to separate the two men. Somehow, in the frenzy, she hit out and the knife plunged into the throat of her lover, John Games.

'Mary Hunter had killed the man she really loved.' Leif glanced down at the painting of the Hunter family. 'Local folk thought she despised and rejected poor Games once the rich suitor from London came along. Nothing she said could convince them otherwise and Squires certainly didn't stand by her even though she'd saved his life because of it. So, the wretched girl was hanged in public and her body displayed on Scurra gibbet. Several days later her family retrieved the body and arranged for a Christian burial on Bolt.'

'It *was* her grave, then?' asked Juliet.

Leif nodded. 'And,' he added. 'According to Stephen Games, the owner of Scurra General Stores and a descendant of John Games, you can still see his ancestor's grave in St Michael's Church. Within a year of the murder, the Hunters had left the island.'

Sir Alec stirred.

'So why is all this relevant?'

'Mary Hunter may have been hanged but she could not rest. She had destroyed the life of the man she had really loved and hated the man who'd led her to this end. Her tormented spirit kept returning, all the time looking for a way she could redeem herself.'

'So?'

'So, every so often guests staying at the hotel, and particularly in Juliet's room, they're disturbed by the ghostly figure. According to the chairman of the Scurra Ghost Club, her visits are infrequent but usually when there is a similar situation to hers.'

'To hers!' exclaimed Sir Alec. 'How in blazes can there be any similarity with Juliet? You're talking nonsense!'

'Listen, Dad,' cut in Juliet. 'Please listen.'

Leif took a deep breath.

212

'Sir Alec,' he continued slowly. 'I know you may have little regard for me. And particularly after what Mr Harrison may have told you.'

'But it's all lies,' protested Juliet. 'Edward's misled you. And he got someone to slash Leif's tent. He . . .'

Leif glanced over to Juliet and she fell silent.

'Sir, I love Juliet,' he continued. 'Just as John Games loved Mary Hunter.'

Sir Alec regarded Leif dubiously.

'And you sir, would like Juliet to marry Edward Harrison just as John Hunter wanted Mary to marry the more distinguished Andrew Squires.'

'That's nonsense!' declared Sir Alec bluntly. 'Juliet is free to marry who she likes.'

'No, Dad,' cut in Juliet. 'It's true. You've put enormous pressure on me to go out with Edward. That's why you invited him to Scurra. It's true Dad, if you're honest. You want me to marry Edward.'

'Well, he'd make you a mighty fine husband. He'll . . .' Sir Alec hesitated a moment and looked back at Leif. 'But how does all this fit in with what happened tonight?'

Leif edged forward in his seat.

'Ever since we arrived at Scurra, Mary Hunter's presence has been getting stronger. And I'm sure that Mary Hunter spotted the similarity between her own tragedy and the position of Juliet. Two men wanting to win her. One impoverished while the other, the man her father would like her to marry, distinguished and with fine prospects ahead of him. But possibly interested in your money as well. Juliet will tell you, Harrison was putting more and more pressure on her, in fact he became obsessive.

'I believe, and so does an islander called Ma Demuth, that Mary Hunter chose to intervene and try to rid herself of some of the guilt that has tormented her for so long. Mary Hunter's intention was to help Juliet and that is why she made attempts to contact us. She wanted us to know she was there.'

'What exactly are you trying to say?'

'Mary Hunter did not want Juliet's life ruined by her being forced into marrying a person she did not really love.' Leif paused. 'And tonight was the conclusion of her legacy.

'In the same room that the murder was committed, I came face to face with Edward Harrison, just as John Games faced Andrew Squires. And just as Games and Squires fought, so did Harrison and I. But this time there was no knife. And Mary Hunter seeking a salvation for her own crime and not wanting Juliet to suffer as she did, appeared in her ghostly form.'

'But Edward is in a state of deep shock,' protested Sir Alec.

Leif nodded. 'I don't know how Mary Hunter looked when she pulled back her hair, but yes, she did frighten Harrison.'

Juliet glanced across at Leif. 'But surely you didn't know Mary Hunter might come? Or that Edward would come into the room?'

'I didn't know about Edward, though you have told me he's entered unannounced before. But I was confident Mary Hunter would appear and that she would somehow try to help. I didn't know how or what exactly would happen, but I believed Mary Hunter was desperate to find a way to redeem herself. She was basically a good honest girl who had no intention of killing Games or anyone else for that matter. It was a tragic accident and she's been in torment ever since. Tonight was a chance for her to help you, Juliet, in a situation so like her own.'

Sir Alec glanced at Leif.

'So,' he started slowly. 'If I am to believe all this, am I also to believe that you are in love with Juliet?'

'Yes, sir.'

'Well, young man,' declared Sir Alec. 'You hardly know each other. You can put that notion right out of your head. You are just not suitable. You have no—'

'But, Dad,' interrupted Juliet. 'Don't you remember, you were once in exactly the same position as Leif? When you were Leif's age you had nothing. No money. No job. But you had determination, Dad, and willpower. So has Leif.'

Leif looked at Sir Alec earnestly.

'Sir, the last thing my father said to me before he died was, "*Du kan gore det, min son, du kan gore det.*" Which means "you can do it, my son, you can do it". And I intend that to be true. And,' added Leif with a smile, 'it is a melancholy truth that even great men have their poor relations.'

Sir Alec looked thoughtfully at Leif. '*Bleak House*?' he queried.

'*Bleak House,*' confirmed Leif.

Juliet smiled. She had forgotten Leif's interest in Victorian literature, but quoting Dickens was a fine way to win her father's approval.

Together, hand in hand, Juliet and Leif made their way across the open expanses of Bolt towards the ruined church. In his free hand, Leif carried a wreath of carnations.

'Your father seems to have taken all this in his stride,' he said.

Juliet nodded. 'He's been remarkable. And he was so relieved when he spoke to the hospital. Edward is much better.' Juliet hesitated. 'I wonder what Mary Hunter looked like when she pulled her hair away from her face.'

'I think it best not to ask. All I could see was her hair, not her face.'

Juliet leaned over and kissed Leif.

'I love you,' she whispered.

Once at the church they made their way to the lonely grave at the back and with the initials MEH still faintly visible on the weathered cross.

'Here,' said Leif, handing the wreath to Juliet.

'We'll put it down together,' she said.

Slowly they advanced towards the old headstone and placed the wreath in front of it.

'May she now rest in peace.'

'And her legacy laid to rest,' added Leif.

They gazed for a few moments at the grave before finally moving away.

ABOUT THE AUTHOR

Neil Somerville was born in Middlesex and has lived in Kent, the Isle of Wight and Berkshire. His mother interested him in writing at an early age and he has gone on to write many bestselling books including *Cat Wisdom: 60 Lessons You Can Learn from a Cat, The Answers,* a long running series on Chinese Horoscopes as well as many popular puzzle books including *The Literary Puzzle Book*. Legacy is his first novel.
Neil is married and has two adult children.

www.neilsomerville.com

Printed in Great Britain
by Amazon